Fusilli Foul Play

A ROMANO'S FAMILY RESTAURANT COZY MYSTERY
BOOK 3

ROSIE A. POINT

Fusilli Foul Play

A Romano's Family Restaurant Cozy Mystery Book 3

Cover by DLR Cover Designs
www.dlrcoverdesigns.com

 Created with Vellum

You're invited!

Hi there, reader!

I'd like to formally invite you to join my awesome community of readers. We love to chat about cozy mysteries, cooking, and pets.

It's super fun because I get to share chapters from yet-to-be-released books, fun recipes, pictures, and do giveaways with the people who enjoy my stories the most.

So whether you're a new reader or you've been enjoying my stories for a while, you can catch up with other like-minded readers, and get lots of cool content by visiting my website at *www.rosiepointbooks.com* and signing up for my mailing list.

Or simply search for me on *www.bookbub.com* and follow me there.

I look forward to getting to know you better.

Let's get into the story!

Yours,
Rosie

One

"There's a woman in the tree."

I stopped halfway through the living room, a moving box clasped in my hands, and stared at my best friend. Matilda had pushed back her gray fringe with a checked scarf, and she had her hands on her hips, her blue-eyed gaze fixed on the trees in the backyard.

"That one there," she said, gesturing out of the floor-to-ceiling windows at the back of Jacob's house. "Down by the water."

The view of Lake Basil was gorgeous, even though fall had officially made its presence known, bringing with it a carpet of brown leaves, brisk winds, and the occasional bruising of the sky—from azure to a deep steely gray.

I put down the box—my old diaries and sentimental items, including my uncle's special recipe book—and cast a weary gaze at Matilda. "I—What? There's a who in the what?"

"There's a girl in the tree. No, not a girl, it's definitely a woman," Matilda said. "I can see her legs dangling from the lowest branch. Right between the foliage."

"Are you having withdrawal symptoms from Jumbo or something?" I walked over to her and feigned taking her temperature. "You want to see a doctor? Smelling burned toast?"

Matilda gave me a good-natured tap on the back of the hand, swatting away my feigned concern. "I'm serious. There's a girl in the tree."

"A who in the what?" That came from my ridiculously handsome chef boyfriend, Jacob, who had just entered the house carrying one of my bags.

"Oh, for goodness' sake," Matilda sighed. "Would you to stop making jokes and just see what I see?" She gestured toward the lake again.

I flashed her a grin and peered down at the placid waters of Lake Basil. I still couldn't believe that today was *the day*. Moving day. Jacob and I had decided to move into his lakeside cabin because it made the most sense. It was a beautiful piece of real estate, even if it did need a bit of work here or there, with a view of the lake. It was the perfect place to retreat to after a long day at the restaurant.

But I was nervous about the move.

This was a big step for us, and it was the reason I'd asked Matilda to come along today to "help me move." Even though I didn't have much to move except a box of old stuff and a few bags. I'd come to Lake Basil with the clothes on my back and my beaten up Honda. And a lot of emotional baggage—but that didn't count when it came to moving, since it was always with me.

Couldn't even breathe without worrying about whether I was too much, too little, or just right. Like the emotional trauma equivalent of *Goldilocks and the Three Bears*.

"See her?" Matilda asked.

I'd been admiring the view. "Uh…"

"Oh, what the heck?" Jacob had left the bag next to his worn leather sofa and stood beside me. "Who is that?"

I came to my senses and scanned the treeline, hurriedly.

There!

A pair of very tan legs dangled from one of the tree branches. It looked as if this woman, she had on glittery pink kicks, had seated her butt in the tree and was facing our way. Toward the house. What was that about?

"I'll go talk to her," I said.

"What if she can't talk?" That came from Matilda.

"Huh?" I frowned, scraping my dark curls into a bun. "What are you—?"

"I mean, what if she's dead?"

Jacob and Matilda exchanged a glance, then looked at me. "I should go out there first," Jacob blustered. "I'm the man of the house. I should—"

"Easy there, cowboy." I patted him on the shoulder. "I'll check it out." I'd dealt with worse than a girl in a tree back in the City. If anyone was going to deal with a female interloper, it was me. "You use those big, strong muscles to get the rest of my bags."

Jacob grinned at me and performed a mock salute. "I see how life is going to be now that we're living together." And then he scooted out of the living room before I could swat him on the backside.

"You watch your mouth, Murphy," I called.

"I don't think anyone's taking this whole 'girl in the tree' issue seriously," Matilda said in a low tone.

"I'm going, I'm going." It was difficult not to be in good spirits now that I'd moved out of my aunt and uncle's house. I adored living with them, and I missed them already, even though I'd seen them not thirty minutes ago, but now I could live guilt-free. I wasn't living off them anymore. I was helping them now.

I exited onto the back porch, the screen door slapping shut behind me, and trudged into the long grass in the backyard.

The legs kicked back and forth, then disappeared from

sight as whoever it was climbed higher into the tree. It was probably a teen messing around with the last couple of warm days in Lake Basil. Enjoying the lake view.

Then why was she facing toward the house?

A passing sense of unease came over me. I shook my head and stopped right underneath the old oak, peering up into the branches.

The woman had tried and failed to hide from view.

She wore a leopard print strappy top and a pair of cut-off jeans.

"Lucia? Lucia, is that you?"

"No."

"Lucia Moretti, I can see you up there," I said. "What the heck do you think you're doing?" Wildin' out was the only right answer in this case.

"It's not me."

"Lucia, if you don't get your butt out of that tree, I'm going to call the cops."

"Yeah nah," Lucia replied, peering down at me through fake lashes and brown eyes. "You ain't gonna do all of that."

"I will. Try me."

Lucia pursed her lips. "This *mad* dumb," she muttered under her breath, before descending from the higher branches. I had to hand it to her. For a thirty-some-thing-year-old woman, she was pretty spry. She reached the final branch, squirmed across it, and then dropped down in front of me. "Look, don't start somethin' and—"

"Start something? You're the one in my tree," I said.

"Ain't your tree."

"Huh?"

"Ain't your tree. That's Jacob's tree, so..."

"Jacob and I are moving in together," I said, the words slipping out of my mouth before I could stop them. Admittedly, it was because I was annoyed with her. And her entire family. The Morettis had come to Lake Basil acting like the typical "cliche" New York Italian family, and it annoyed not just me, but every other Lake Basilite. We were all New York Italians and nobody *acted* like that. It just wasn't a thing.

Easy. Put the rage aside. "Look, you've got like," I broke off, making a show out of checking my watch, "five seconds to get off this property before I call the police."

"Whatever," Lucia said. "I was just hanging out. Don't make it into something weird." And then she trudged toward the lake shore. She hovered for a second, glaring at me, before heading down the embankment and disappearing from sight.

"What was that about?" Jacob called from the back porch.

"I have no idea," I said.

And I wasn't sure I wanted to find out.

6

Two

The following morning...

MOVING IN TOGETHER WASN'T THE ONLY THING
that was changing in my life. The restaurant was getting a
revamp—not the aesthetic revamp and relaunch that we'd
done this summer, but new staff members. Business was
better than it had ever been, and with the tourist season
slowly dropping off, now was the time to take stock, hire
new staff, and figure out who stayed, who would go, and
where we were headed.

All big and scary things to think about for any business
person.

"Ready to start?" Jacob asked, pressing a hand to the
small of my back.

I stood behind the reception desk in the restaurant, my finger trailing down the long list of applicants who were due for interviews with us today. We were looking for a new sous chef, and Jacob had to be here to see how they performed.

"Uh…" I opened my mouth to tell him that I was worried, nervous even to make another big step, but thought better of it. "I'm fine."

"Gina."

"What?"

"You know you can rely on me, right?"

"Sure." I gave him a sweet smile, but didn't open up about what I was feeling. Honestly, I still found it mad hard to open up to anyone, even Matilda and Jumbo. It was even worse trying to rely on others. So far, I'd only been let down, and in business and my personal life, I wanted to dig my fingers in and hang on until my knuckles turned white.

That way I could control what went right. And take the blame for when things went wrong.

"I'm just saying," Jacob started.

"Seriously, I'm fine." I gave him a warm smile so that he wouldn't take it to heart. "Just focused on moving forward with the business and our lives." Definitely not terrified of the fact that we were living together and that I could mess this up easily. When it came to restaurants, I was confident, but with relationships—

"Did you find out why Lucia was in the back yard yesterday?" Jacob asked.

My gaze snapped to his face, and my heart fluttered despite the question having nothing to do with romance. The man was handsome, ridiculously so, and he flashed me a grin that dimpled his cheeks when he noticed my scrutiny. "Why do you ask?"

"Because last night, I could have sworn that I heard—"

A knock rattled the glass front door of Romano's Family Restaurant, and a guy with a fuzz of dark hair over his head and extra around the middle waved at us from the street.

This was our first interview.

Jacob called the guy inside. "Mr. Marino," Jacob said, rounding the walnut reception desk and sticking out a hand.

The two men gave each other a serious-faced handshake. "Nice to meet you, sir," Mr. Marino said. "You must be the head chef, that right?"

"That's right. Come on over and sit down." Jacob gestured to one of the tables. We usually left the chairs upside down atop them, but Jacob had already brought three down for our interviews today.

"Mr. Marino." I shook our applicant's hand. His palm

was clammy, and his gaze skittered left and right from my face to Jacob's. "I'm Gina Romano, the owner."

"Right, right, I heard all about you," Mr. Marino said. "You can call me Leo, by the way. I appreciate you accepting my application for an interview, or whatever you call that." He gave an awkward laugh. "And that you let me come in first. I got a job at the moment, and I don't really want my boss knowing that I'm down here."

I understood what it was like, looking for new employment, but the honesty was refreshing. "Who do you work for?" I asked.

Leo licked his thick lips, glanced back over his shoulder. "I gotta say?"

"Not if it makes you uncomfortable," I replied smoothly. "I'd much rather talk about what you can offer to Romano's. And there's the matter of your resume." I shifted my tablet onto the desk—I'd bought one recently for business and it had been a game changer for the restaurant. I opened the resume he'd emailed to my business account. I pressed the tablet across the table toward Jacob so that he could see the screen.

"I was impressed by your qualifications," Jacob said. "And your experience. You've been doing this long enough to secure a head chef position at a restaurant in the City, let alone in this town. Why do you want the position of sous chef?"

Leo sniffed. "Well, you see, I prefer it that way. I like what I do, but I prefer not to be the guy at the top. I've had some experience with that, and it's not for me. What can I say? I'm not that kind of guy."

"But you'd say you're good at delegating tasks?" Jacob asked.

"Oh yeah, of course. No problem."

I listened to them talk—I wanted Jacob to take the lead on this because he was my head chef and I trusted his choices when it came to the kitchen and its staff. It was important to empower him so that he could produce the best meals possible for our customers. Breathing down his neck and micromanaging him wouldn't get us there.

Besides, this gave me an opportunity to watch Mr. Marino and how he interacted with Jacob.

There was something... strange about his behavior. First interview nerves? Maybe. But the way he kept glancing back at the door, almost as if he expected to be caught in this interview?

Jacob's questions lulled, so I stepped in. "This is all great, Leo," I said. "We'll have to get you into the kitchen for a trial run, but I had a question."

"Sure."

"What's with the gap in your resume?" I asked. "It says here that you were working at Grazing Getty out in Branford until the end of last summer. Then what?"

"I, uh, I had some family issues to attend to," Leo said. "And after that, uh—"

"After that, he started working for my sister." Romeo Moretti's voice snapped through the interior of the restaurant. He'd entered quietly, and he held the door open halfway, a breeze chasing in after him. "You no good, piece of trash." Romeo was already rolling up the sleeves of his buttoned shirt. "Why, I ought to knock your teeth in for this. You going behind my sister's back? To her main competitors?"

I rose from my seat. "Mr. Moretti, you need to leave." I was going to try my hardest to be civil with the man, even though he irritated me right to my core, from the dark hair parted perfectly to one side, to the way he puffed out his chest and swaggered around Lake Basil, acting like he owned the place.

Jacob got up too, eyes narrowing. Jacob was a pretty calm dude most of the time, but Romeo got on his nerves. The only person who irritated him more was the local detective, Shawn Carter.

"I should go," Leo said. "I didn't mean to cause no trouble."

"Yeah, you get outta here." Romeo made a grab for the chef as he hurried past, but Leo escaped Romeo's outstretched hand by ducking to one side. Moretti turned toward us. "You trying to steal my sister's chef, huh? That's low, Romano, even for you."

"Get out," Jacob said. "Now. Before we call the cops."

Romeo backed up, opening the door. "You're gonna pay for this, Romano," he said, pointing at me. "I'm gonna make you pay." And then he dipped out of sight.

Three

At this point, I knew better than to take Romeo's words at face-value. The man had a habit of bandying about threats like he was sprinkling cheese over a pie, and I was over worrying about *his next move*. Especially since he hadn't made any moves over the last half of the summer.

He was irrelevant to our business plans and our lives. Besides, if Lucia had a problem with us interviewing her chef, then she had to take it up with us, not send her gorilla of a brother over.

I sighed, marking my place in my paperback with my finger.

Jacob had already gone up to bed, but I had opted to stay downstairs in the kitchen with a glass of hot chocolate and a good book.

It was past eleven, and I couldn't sleep. Things had changed so much for me over the last year, and with the restaurant succeeding and my life starting with Jacob, I should have been happy. But a deep sense of unease had settled into place in my belly, and I couldn't figure out what was bugging me.

Maybe it was the change.

Or maybe it was the fact that I had clawed my way back from the jaws of defeat.

I took another sip of hot chocolate and swirled my cup. I was almost done, and then I'd have to make another attempt at sleep.

Jacob's kitchen had brought me a measure of comfort —it wasn't as cozy as Aunt Sof's, but it was still warm and—

A thump in the house stilled my thoughts.

I listened hard, hyper-focusing.

Relax. It was nothing. Just the wind.

I shifted my bookmark into my paperback and started to rise from the creaky kitchen chair when—

Another thump.

This one had sounded louder, closer to the back of the house? Closer to where I sat right now. My heart pitter-pattered out a rhythm in my chest, and I abandoned my mug and book, pressing myself to the kitchen wall.

I hit the lights.

The sudden darkness toyed with my depth perception, and I felt my way out of the kitchen and into the hallway. I'd left my phone on my bedside table. I needed it to call the police if anything weird happened.

You're imagining it. Everything's fine. You're tired.

But Uncle Rocco had taught me to trust my instincts in both life and business, and I wasn't about to stop now.

I started up the stairs, sticking to the edge closest to the wall to make the least amount of noise possible. If there was someone out there, I didn't want them to see me. What if they had a gun? What if—?

The shattering of glass broke the quiet, and I ran the rest of the way up the stairs.

I skidded down the hall and through the bedroom doorway and collided with something heavy and warm.

I screeched.

"Gina," Jacob said. "Relax. It's just me."

I gasped, shuddering. What was wrong with me? I'd totally forgotten that Jacob was in the house in the first place. And it was *his* house.

"There's someone breaking in," I said. "Downstairs."

"Stay here," Jacob said, and re-entered the bedroom. He came out with a baseball bat that gave me a shiver. Not so long ago, a man had been murdered by a baseball-bat wielding psychopath.

"I can't let you go down there alone." The crunch of

glass sent another thrill of alarm through my core. "I'm calling the cops." I rushed into the bedroom, fully expecting that Jacob would wait for me before he did anything.

The person breaking in could have a knife or a gun. There was no sense putting himself in danger.

I grabbed my phone and unlocked it, hurriedly typing in the emergency numbers as I strode back toward the second-floor hallway. Jacob was gone.

"Jake," I hissed into the darkness. "Jacob, where are you? Jake?"

A silence.

My finger dipped toward the green phone icon on my screen and—

"Down here," Jacob called, his voice full of mirth. "Gina, you're not going to believe this."

"Huh?"

The downstairs hall light clicked on, and Jacob reappeared. "Come on downstairs to the study. You don't have to call the cops."

"Why?" I tucked my phone into the pocket of my fluffy pink robe and descended to meet him, taking his hand. "Whats' going on?"

Jacob led me into the study, where the lights were on, and a vase lay shattered on the floor. The window beside the door that led out onto the side of the house was open.

A black cat, its fur standing all on end, had latched its claws into the curtain beside the window.

"Just a cat," Jacob said. "I think it got spooked and knocked the vase over." He gestured to the desk that held his computer and my tablet.

I sighed, hugging my body. "I could have sworn..."

Jacob chuckled. "Just a scared kitty."

I reached up and carefully unhooked the cat's claws. It made a great show of hissing at me, and the minute I got it down, it leaped out of my arms and back through the open window.

"I don't like it," I whispered.

"What?" Jacob asked as he closed the window. "Careful of your bare feet. The glass is everywhere."

"Did you open the window?"

"Not that I recall, but we've been kind of busy lately."

"And where did the cat come from? Do your neighbors have a cat?"

"Might be a stray," Jacob said. "Stay here. I'm going to get the dustpan. Careful of your feet."

I gnawed on the inside of my cheek. The more I thought about it, the more this didn't seem right. The window open when Jacob didn't remember opening it, the vase broken, and the cat that was spooked. Why was it afraid? Cats weren't clumsy. And the vase had been positioned on a shelf near the window. One that was within reach of—

My eyes widened, and I hurried over to the bookcase where I had stored my Uncle Rocco's recipe book, full of his top secret recipes for the most delicious dishes at the restaurant.

I ran my fingers over the spines, my pulse hammering.

It was gone.

The recipe book was gone.

"Gina? You—?"

"Lucia Moretti," I hissed.

"Uh...? No, I'm Jacob. Your live-in boyfriend, remember?" He grinned at me from where he swept up the glass beside the shelf.

"No. Lucia Moretti stole my uncle's recipe book. The recipe book that held this week's special."

"The fusilli?"

"Yeah! She took it," I said. "That's why she was hanging around down by the lake, spying on us the other day." I gritted my teeth.

"Relax, Gina, you don't know if she did this."

"I'm pretty darn sure," I said. "And I'm going to make her give me that recipe book back in person tomorrow."

"If it's gone, you should report it stolen."

"That too," I said, not that I'd had great experiences

with the cops in this town. But Jacob had a point. "But will they take it seriously?"

"You're going to have to call Shawn over here." Jacob didn't sound happy about it.

"You know what? No. I'm going to handle this myself. I know for sure it was Lucia, and I'm going to make her rue the day she decided to mess with us."

He finished cleaning up and then came over, placing an arm around my waist. "Come on, now. Come on to bed and sleep. We can deal with this in the morning."

"Thanks for cleaning up," I said absently.

I doubted I would get a wink of sleep tonight.

Four

The following morning...

"AUNT SOF?" I BANGED ON THE FRONT DOOR LIKE
a woman possessed first thing the next morning. "Aunt
Sof, are you awake? I need to talk to you?"

Footsteps clattered toward the front door, and I shook
my head at myself for coming by this early. But Aunt Sofia
was usually awake before I was, up and making something
scrumptious for breakfast to keep my uncle happy.
Cooking was Aunt Sofia's love language.

The door latch clacked and my aunt peered out at me,
wide-eyed, her dark frizzy hair streaked with gray but tied
back into a cute bun.

"Gina? Back already? Don't tell me you and Jacob had
a fight?" She looked utterly crestfallen at the idea.

"We didn't have a fight," I said.

"Oh thank goodness." My dear aunt ushered me into the cramped hall of my childhood home, and I was instantly assaulted by the familiarity and the warmth of coming home. It was silly—I'd barely left, literally a day or two ago—but I already missed this place.

"I would hate it if you two fought," Aunt Sofia said, walking ahead of me. "I firmly believe that you were made for each other. But then, there's always that Shawn Carter if things fall through with Jacob."

"Auntie!"

"What?" she asked innocently. "It's good to keep one's options open. Besides, that's a good way to keep a man on his toes, you know?"

"What is?"

"If they think there's another man who's interested, well, they'll make sure that they always treat you right." Aunt Sofia fixed me a mug of coffee and settled me at the table. "Now, what's got you so antsy? You look like you're about to jump out of your skin."

I told her about the break-in last night while I sipped on the coffee—not a great choice since I was already keyed up—and how I was convinced that it was Lucia who'd stolen the book.

"That's terrible," Aunt Sofia whispered, lifting her apron onto her head. It was dotted with sunflowers, and she brushed her palms over it as she spoke. "You can't tell your uncle. He'll lose it if he finds out someone took his recipe book. That was a special gift for your eyes only."

"I know," I said. "But don't worry, Auntie, I'm going to get it back, even if I have to wrangle it from Lucia's cold, dead fingers."

"Gina! You know better than to talk like that. Goodness."

My aunt was right. I was angry, not only about the fact that Lucia had been watching us and had stolen the recipe book, but that she'd caused so much trouble in Lake Basil in the first place.

"Sorry," I said, after a beat. "We've just moved in together and started getting settled and then this happens. I mean, that book means everything to me. And we use the recipes in it too, you know?"

"You don't have a copy of it?"

"I saved digital copies to my tablet," I said, "so we'll be able to go ahead with the special, but what's the point when Lucia can use the recipes to make her own competing special?"

Aunt Sofia had started whipping up pancake batter, and she stirred it, the bowl propped on her hip as we talked. "What does Jacob say about all of this?"

"He said we should talk to Shawn," I replied. "Even though he doesn't particularly like the guy, and that's sensible, but I don't want to make a big fuss out of this when I can handle it myself."

Aunt Sofia pursed her lips. "Sounds like you *want* to handle it yourself."

Nobody could accuse me of not having a temper. Sure, I tried to stay calm most of the time but when someone messed with my family or friends, the people I loved, then the city girl in me came out and I was ready to go to war.

Aunt Sofia set the bowl aside and fisted her hips. "I'll help you," she said, "but we've got to keep this a secret from Rocky."

"No problem," I said, "but I don't want you getting involved, Auntie. This could be dangerous."

"Nonsense. It's Lucia Moretti. Besides, I know a few things about her that might help you." My aunt was the gossip in chief in Lake Basil. She spent a lot of her time on the phone gossiping, or down at the salon doing the same. For a woman who loved avoiding painful topics, she was somewhat of a gossip connoisseur.

"Like what?" I asked, and then I pulled a face. "Do I want to know?"

"Sure you do," Aunt Sofia said. "I know she's been dating around a lot. There are a lot of guys who are interested in her, which makes sense because she's a pretty girl. Bit mouthy, but pretty."

"I'm not sure that's going to help me with finding the recipe book. Short of going down to her restaurant—"

"You wouldn't find her there even if you did," Aunt Sofia said, with a wriggle of her expressive eyebrows.

"Oh yeah?"

"What's today? A Tuesday?" Aunt Sofia waited for my nod in the affirmative before continuing. "Then she's not down at the restaurant. She's up at the Moretti mansion with Stretchy McGee."

"And what, may I ask, is a Stretchy McGee? Is that some kind of cocktail?"

"No," Aunt Sofia said, with a horrified expression— even the thought of casual day drinking was too much for her. "You know Stretchy. You went to school with her."

"I did?"

"Yes, of course. You know, that short girl with the red hair. She acted in that Shakespearean play the one year?"

"Lavender?" I'd forgotten her last name. "Are you talking about Lavender?"

"That's her. Lavender McGee. Except she's not Lavender anymore. She's Stretchy now," Aunt Sofia said. "Because she's the town yoga instructor. She's very pricey." Aunt Sofia made a face that said, "but that's none of my business." "But apparently, she's very good at what she does, you know. All the wealthy folks hire her. My friend

Desiree said that her hip feels better than it has in years, thanks to her."

"OK," I said, "but what's Stretchy got to do with Lucia?"

"Well, Stretchy teaches Lucia yoga every Tuesday morning," Aunt Sof said. "I know this because Batilda at the salon said that she had to reschedule her yoga class with Stretchy because Lucia threw a temper tantrum about the fact that Stretchy couldn't do yoga with *her* on a Tuesday. And then offered Stretchy a fat wad of cash."

"Who did? Lucia?"

"Yeah." Aunt Sof picked up the bowl of pancake batter again. "But you can — Wait, where are you going?"

"I'm going to find Lucia and get the recipe book back."

"But the pancakes!" My aunt's call followed me down the hallway.

"I love you! I'll drop by later."

"I'll put some in a tupperware for you and Jacob. I hope he likes chocolate chip."

Five

THE MORETTI MANSION WAS TUCKED AWAY IN the "rich" area of Lake Basil, the one that was further back from the Lake, but still within proximity—with enough land to accommodate the fabulous three-story mansion that sprawled its grounds.

When I'd first seen this place, I'd been so invested in figuring out what had happened in a mystery that I hadn't *really* taken it in all its glory. Stone columns, a massive gate, a sweeping lawn and columns at the front of the house. There were always plenty of cars parked out front, but today, there was only one.

Lucia's red sports car.

Just how did the Moretti family afford all of this? There were rumors. Vicious ones about them having been involved in high-end crime back in the City, but none of it was proven. Romeo ran with a "bad" crowd, even if the local police hadn't done anything about it.

I frowned up at the fabulous house.

The gates were open, as if someone had just left, but the house seemed awfully quiet.

Lucia, hold on to your butt. It was about to get serious.

The woman could drive as many sports cars as she wanted, but she couldn't come up with great recipes, or even have her chefs create ones that were good enough to eat. Money didn't buy brains—as cruel as that thought was.

I started up the long path toward the grand front porch, the gravel crunching underfoot as I strode toward the doors.

The closer I drew, the more curious I became. The doors were open a crack. What was that about?

"Hello?" I called out. "Anyone home?"

I should have pressed the intercom at the front gate before coming up here, but that definitely wasn't my style. I was an "act now, ask questions later" kind of gal. I started up the steps—the Morettis surely had a housekeeper or a personal chef. There had to be *someone* here who could tell me where Lucia had gone.

And if not...

I considered sneaking in and trying to find the recipe book without asking.

That was fair, wasn't it? Lucia had stolen it directly from my home. Opened the window and broken a vase in her haste to get her glamorous glittery nail-tipped fingers on the recipe book. She wouldn't have the moral high-ground if I decided to take the recipe book back.

"Lucia?" I called out.

Aunt Sof had said that Lavender—or Stretchy as she was now called—would be up here with Lucia, the pair of them doing yoga.

I reached the front door and nudged it open with the toe of my sneaker. "Lucia?"

Nothing.

I had never been inside the Moretti mansion before, and the minute I stepped over the threshold, my jaw dropped.

The house was *opulent* to say the least. And garishly decorated in golds and crimsons. The dark wood walls held pictures of the family, in various poses, most of them centering around a gray-haired patriarch I didn't recognize.

It felt as if I'd stepped into the lion's den rather than being the lioness on a hunt.

"Lucia?" I called. "Are you in here?"

Soft footfalls drew me through the foyer and toward a massive hallway that held a grand staircase off to one side, and several dark doors on the other, each decoratively carved with the Moretti name.

One of those doors was ajar.

"Lucia?"

I moved toward it, and goosebumps thrilled over my skin. This was wrong. Something was very wrong about this scenario.

"Lucia? Lavender?" I couldn't bring myself to yell out the word "stretchy" into the ostentatious mansion.

I reached the door and bumped it open with my elbow.

The room was just as opulent as the rest of the house, with a thick red carpet that did little to hide the blood. Lucia Moretti lay face down on the carpet, a knife sticking out of her back, and I stared at her for a good few minutes before the reality of the situation could sink in enough for me to move.

I backed up then stopped, horror creeping up my throat.

Lucia was dead.

So very dead.

There was too much blood for her to be anything other than dead, but...

I entered the room, stepping around her body and being careful not to touch anything. I bent beside her and pressed two fingers to her neck, just to be sure. This close, I could make out a curving letter "M" had been carved into the hilt of the silver knife.

Again, I rose and exited the room, not touching the door in case there were fingerprints on it.

This wasn't the first time I had seen a dead body, but this was *Lucia*. The same Lucia who I'd been mad at not ten minutes ago.

I brought my phone out of my purse hurriedly and called 911.

Six

SHAWN CARTER, THOUGH HE COULD BE FULL OF bravado and a bit of a tool on occasion, always did a great job of being comforting when something truly evil had happened. He brought me out onto the front porch and sat me down on the grand steps while the police secured the scene.

"I can't believe this is happening again," I whispered. "Again."

Shawn sat beside me, his notepad and pen out, and his body angled toward mine. "Gina, I'm going to need you to take a deep breath here. I understand this is upsetting, but I need you to go through a few things with me again, all right?"

"Yeah, Shawn, I get it."

"Look, I'm not trying to give you the fifth degree here,

but I've gotta do my job, and you were at the scene. So..."

"Huh? I know. I'll try to help in whatever way I can."

"Great. That's great, Gina." Shawn hesitated.

My gaze moved over the lawn, and it felt as if my brain had dissociated from my body. Maybe that was just the stress talking. "I can't believe it," I said again. "It's Lucia, you know? She hasn't been here that long, but it's still... It's Lucia."

"I heard that you two hadn't been getting along."

I gave Shawn a withering look. "You know very well that we weren't getting along. We'd only just struck up a truce."

Shawn nodded. "That must have been tough."

"It wasn't tough. The fact that she stole my uncle's top secret recipe book was tough."

"Is that why you came out here today?"

"I told you that," I said.

"Right, so you came out here to confront Lucia," Shawn said. "But here's the thing I don't get, Gina. Why'd you go inside?"

"Because nobody was answering the door."

Shawn pulled up his pants legs and considered me. He was broad-shouldered and had been a force to be reckoned with on the football field back in our years at Lake Basil High. Now, he was balding, kind, good-looking, but too pushy. He liked to get his way, Shawn, and if that meant pigeon-holing me into the "person of interest" bucket then he'd have to think again.

"What are you insinuating?" I asked irritably. "That I arrived here seeking revenge for the stolen recipe book, then promptly went ahead and murdered Lucia with a knife from her own kitchen and just called the cops right after?"

"It's been done before," Shawn said. "How did you know the knife was from the kitchen?"

"I didn't. I just saw that it had a letter 'M' etched into the hilt and figured that it must be from their kitchen."

"The Moretti's kitchen?"

"Yes," I said. "Shawn, I didn't do anything. In fact, I thought I was going to catch Lucia doing yoga up here with Lavender McGee, and confront her about the book, get it back, and move on with my life."

"Stretchy McGee?"

"Yes," I said with a long-suffering sigh. "My aunt told me that Lucia does yoga with Lavender on a Tuesday."

Shawn tapped his chin with the end of his pen. "You seem to know a lot about Lucia."

"Oh get real, Shawn. As if I would throw my life away by murdering Lucia. Or anyone for that matter. You really think I'm that bad of a person that I would kill her?" Tears welled up in my eyes as the gravity of the situation hit home.

Lucia was dead.

She hadn't been my friend. She'd made me downright uncomfortable, but she'd still been a part of Lake Basil. Gosh, I hadn't even wanted her to be a part of it, but she'd wormed her way in, and now she was dead.

"How come you were asking after Lucia?" Shawn asked.

"Because of the darn recipe book," I said, heat crawling up my throat. "I swear, how many more times do I have to say it? Shawn, can I take a breather here? I'm starting to get really angry, and I don't want to be rude."

Shawn rose from the steps. "Sure thing, Gina," he said. "But stay right where you are. I've got more questions for you."

He entered the house, and I sat on the front porch under the watchful eye of a nearby officer. I didn't offer him a smile, simply because I was in a foul mood. I was starting to get emotional whiplash from this.

First the big move, then the stolen recipe book, and now Lucia Moretti dead.

A lone figure appeared at the end of the driveway, and the police officer turned toward her, frowning.

She hobbled up, wearing a neatly pressed skirt and blouse, carrying her handbag over one arm and umbrella over the other.

"Excuse me, ma'am, you can't come past this point."

"What's going on?" the woman asked. "I—I'm late for work." She drew herself up straight. "Mr. Moretti will be furious if I don't get the house clean, so you had better move out of my way."

"I'm afraid you don't understand, ma'am," the officer said. "This is a crime scene."

"A crime scene?" The lady frowned. "Nonsense. This is—"

Shawn appeared and strode down the steps toward the woman. "Can I help you ma'am?"

"Yes. You can let me by. I'm the housekeeper, and I—"

"I'm afraid you can't come into the house. We've already notified the owners, but there has been a murder."

"A what?" The woman blinked, her eyes going owlish. She was so small, she could easily have posed as a tawny owl, and the image helped snap me out of my milieu of unhappiness. This poor woman had come to work only to find a disaster.

But what if she was already here and left?

My heart skipped a beat.

Shawn placated the woman and sent her off with the officer, heading back down toward the exit, then came over to me again.

"I'm going to ask you to leave before Romeo and the other Morettis get here," Shawn said. "I know that would be an uncomfortable experience for you."

That was putting it lightly. "Thanks. I appreciate that. Sorry I got so heated."

"Emotions run high when it comes to this kind of thing," Shawn said. "One last thing before you go, Gina?"

"Sure. What's up?"

"Did you see anything suspicious when you came up to the house? Anyone hanging around?" Shawn asked.

"No, nothing," I said. "Just that the front door was open and—"

"What? What is it?"

"I heard footsteps," I said. "Footsteps in the house. I wasn't sure if I imagined them, but yeah, definitely. The sound of someone walking after I called out Lucia's name."

Shawn's eyebrow arched upward. "You're positive?"

"Yes," I said. "And that has to mean..." I paled. "That means the killer was in the house when I was."

Shawn didn't confirm whether he thought the same thing as me. Instead, he sent me on my way with a promise that he had it *all under control.* And a warning that I had better not leave town.

Seven

Romano's Family Restaurant was alive with gossip that night. Now that tourist season had died down, there were more locals dining in the restaurant, and that meant there was more room for small town chitter-chatter. Including news about the murder at the Moretti mansion.

I was doing my best to ignore it, partly because I was naturally intrigued by mysteries, and partly because thinking about how Lucia had died made me sick to my stomach.

I'd done the right thing by checking on her, but it haunted me. I had been so close to the killer, and she had been... well, dead. Dead and only moments before I had walked into that house.

Or had it happened long ago?

I shut my eyes for a moment, standing behind the

reception desk in the bustling restaurant. Had her neck been warm?

It was literally the creepiest thought that had entered my head in my entire life.

But it was important.

Had Lucia's throat been warm when I'd placed my fingers against it? No, not particularly. But it hadn't been ice cold either. Just how long did a body take to cool down after something like that happened?

I shuddered and exhaled, opening my eyes.

I had to let this go.

"It has a ring to it, don't you think?" A customer said at the table closest to the front of the restaurant. Those tables had the best view of the street outside, which was dark. A moonless night to match the mood of the day. The clouds had rolled in, bringing a cold fall wind and the promise of rain late into the night.

That was what the weatherman had said, anyway, but who could trust them?

"What has?" another customer asked—I recognized Natalie from the antique store. She was one of Aunt Sof's friends, and another of those gossips who couldn't enjoy a meal without a side of juicy news.

"The murder at the Moretti mansion," her dinner companion, Joel, said, flicking his hands as if picturing the words in lights. "It could be the title of a movie, or, uh, one of those mystery novels. Stabbed in her own home."

"It's a terrible thing to have happened," Natalie said. "I can scarcely believe it."

"Oh, come on," Joel said. "Seriously? You can't believe it? Everybody hated the woman."

"Joel, that's trashy. Don't talk about the dead like that."

"Trashy or not, it's true. Lucia acted like she owned everyone and everything," he said, checking his nails and sitting back in the comfy dining chair.

I'd made darn sure our dining chairs were comfy. Nothing worse than trying to enjoy your fusilli special in a chair that made your back ache.

"You would act like that too if you had that much money."

Joel clicked his fingers, pressing his glasses up his nose with his middle finger right after. "That's another thing. Where'd she get all the money from, huh? That whole family's suspicious."

"I heard Romeo's been making all the bad kinds of friends," Natalie said.

"Mm-hmm." Joel took a sip of his wine, swirling the glass like he was a soothsayer over a cauldron. "And they're not the only ones who would've wanted Lucia out of the way."

"Who else?" For all her protestations, Natalie sure looked invested in this conversation.

Joel took a long sip of his wine, his gaze flickering around the room, and I quickly averted my eyes. I'd been unashamedly eavesdropping on their conversation—and I didn't plan to stop. I'd just be less obvious about it.

"Alls I'm saying is that if I was Stretchy McGee, I'd be schvitzing right about now. Or packing to get the heck out of dodge before it was too late," Joel said.

"Too late?"

"The cops are going to be knocking on her door," Joel said. "I heard she was the last one to see Lucia alive."

"Yeah, but you don't know that for sure."

"She's mad suspicious," Joel said. "Bet. She's the one who did this. Besides, surely you've heard the rumors about her temper."

"No?" Natalie leaned forward, spilling her white wine onto the tablecloth and hastily dabbing it up with her handkerchief. "She had a temper?"

"Oh yeah. Apparently, she was seeing a big therapist out in the City. Like she was doing those online therapy calls because she needed anger management so bad," Joel said. "Liable to snap at any moment."

Now, that *was* interesting.

"That's terrible."

"And ironic," Joel said, with another sip of wine. He

smacked his lips with relish. "The yoga instructor losing her temper and killing her highest paying client? I mean, come on. Someone should pay me to write this screenplay."

It *was* ironic.

But was it true? That was the question.

There were too many strange goings-on in Lake Basil. First, Lucia had been hiding in my tree and now this. And I didn't have the recipe book back either. And then there was Romeo Moretti and the way he'd acted when he'd seen Lucia's chef in an interview with us for the job here.

I sighed. I'd have to let Leo down gently. He'd been unable to bring Lucia's restaurant up to par as the head chef, and I'd smelled the burned garlic when I'd gone in there to see what the place was about.

Not that it mattered at this point.

A woman was dead, and that *had* to be the main concern.

If there was a killer on the loose then—

The front door of the restaurant opened, and a pretty woman in her thirties entered. She was instantly familiar, shorter than me with red frizzy hair. She bore a smile that seemed almost too big for her deeply tan face.

Instantly, all noise in the restaurant stopped, apart from the gentle tinkle of Italian lounge music from the stereos seated against the brick walls.

Forks dropped to plates. Heads turned.

Lavender McGee smiled, clearly oblivious as to why everyone had stopped eating.

She came toward the reception area, and the noise slowly resumed.

"Good evening, ma'am," I said, "how may I—?"

"Gina? Gina Romano, is that you?"

"Lavender?" I feigned recognition. "Oh wow, hi! I haven't seen you in years? How have you been holding up?"

"Oh, you can call me Stretchy," she said. "Everyone else does. I'm a yoga instructor now, and the nickname kind of stuck. I like it better than Lavender, anyway. But yeah, I'm great." She rounded the desk and drew me into a hug that drew more attention from the diners. "Oh my gosh, how nice to see you again. Been for ages and for ever!"

"Nice to see you too." I patted her on the back awkwardly. Lavender and I hadn't exactly been friends in high school. Sure, she hadn't been a bully like Brittany Brown, but we had barely exchanged a couple of words.

"Well, don't you look radiant," Lavender said, fluttering her eyelashes at me. "My goodness, you've really got a glow." She said that last part loudly, and glanced left toward the room full of diners.

Ah. So that's her game. She was trying to act sweet and

43

nice in front of the others. "Thanks," I said. "Say, I've been thinking about taking some couples yoga classes. Do you offer something like that?"

"I sure do. In fact, I've just had a slot open up. Are you free next Tuesday?"

My insides curled. "Absolutely," I said. "Table for one?"

"Oh yes. Just for one."

Eight

The following Tuesday...

"I CAN'T *BELIEVE* THAT YOU SIGNED US UP FOR this," Jacob said.

"It'll be great," I said. "There's nothing quite as refreshing as doing yoga with a potential murderer. You'll see. A great combination of relaxation and utter terror. Like tenderizing meat."

"Well, now that you put it *that* way." Jacob grinned at me, then looped his arm around my waist and pulled me into a hug. "Are you sure you want to do this?"

"Absolutely."

I'd spent the week leading up to today busy with everything other than worrying about the murder. That wasn't *strictly* true. The murder had been on my mind a lot, as had the recipe book. Shawn had dropped by Jacob's house to ask me why I hadn't laid a report about the missing recipe book in the first place, and that had been a *fun* conversation.

I loved explaining to Shawn that the reason I didn't want to tell him was because I'd figured I'd find the book faster than he could.

And then there had been hiring a new sous chef, letting down the others we'd tested, and catching up with Matilda and Jumbo. Also, trying to find the recipe book had provided more difficulty than I'd anticipated.

The Morettis weren't talking to anybody. Their restaurant was closed. And there were no leads apart from Lucia herself having stolen it or it being Stretchy.

And aside from all of that, living with Jacob had presented us with new problems—namely, the black cat who had started frequenting our house.

He wasn't so much a problem as he was an adorable perk. But Jacob was averse to adopting him.

We got into Jacob's car and took the long drive down to the park where we had our "meeting" with Lavender McGee.

"You really think this woman might have murdered Lucia?" Jacob asked.

"I don't know. Maybe." I gave Jacob a tight-lipped smile.

I loved that he was doing this with me, but it had been silly of me to involve him. I'd opted for couples yoga because it was safer. If Lavender was a murderer, I didn't particularly want to do yoga alone with her, especially if she'd been at the Moretti mansion and heard me calling out to Lucia.

But now, I had second thoughts. I didn't want Jacob getting involved, or worse, getting hurt because of my decision.

Lake Basil had a couple of parks, but the one we'd agreed on was the most central, closest to the restaurants and coffee shops. Trees dotted the park, their leaves in reds and browns and the warm gold of fall, and Lavender stood out among them in her pink sports bra and yoga pants.

She waved us over excitedly.

"There you are," she cried, bobbing up and down, her red ponytail hopping in time with the movements. "Are you two ready to do some yoga?" She clapped her hands, gesturing for us to come over.

"I thought yoga was meant to be relaxing," Jacob murmured.

"Tenderizing meat, remember?"

He shot me a dubious look.

We joined Lavender in the middle of the park, in full view of the lazy path that wandered through it, along with the benches that were blessedly empty. "I thought you might not have yoga mats so I brought some along."

Three mats had been laid out on the grass—two greens and a purple. Lavender directed us to them, grinning from ear-to-eat. "It's so good to have a new client. I just lost my previous one."

"I heard about that," I said. "Lucia?"

"That's right," Lavender said cheerfully. "Now, you two just follow along. We're going to start with some deep breathing first, and then I'm going to have you hang heavy, just like this." She hinged forward, dropping her head toward the ground but kept her knees soft.

"I don't think I can do that," Jacob said. "My legs won't... let me." He grunted, lowering himself. "Oh hey, nevermind. I think I've got it."

"Impressive," I said. "Flexible for a highly strung chef."

Jacob shot me a mutinous look from between his knees, and I held back a giggle. I dropped down into the same position. "I heard Lucia was stabbed," I said, as we hung suspended.

"That's correct," Lavender sang, still in that jarringly cheerful tone. "Stabbed right in the back according to the police. I saw it coming, didn't you?"

"No?"

"Oh, come on, Gina," Lavender said. "You know what she was like. Lucia was the type of woman who liked to bully others. Just like Brittany. And straighten and reach your hands up above your head." She did exactly that, stretching high. "And let them drop."

We followed her directions, trying to breathe like she did. But I could hardly concentrate on doing yoga. "You didn't like Lucia?"

"I don't think I know a person who did," Lavender said. "She insisted on calling me by my first name rather than my nickname even though I asked several times." The way she worded "several times" was emphatic, and Lavender's cheeks had grown pink. "It's ridiculous, but I guess that's how these City folk like to behave. No offense."

"None taken." She put us in a side stretch.

"Really try to reach out overhead. That's right, and now just a slight rotation of the ribs upward to the sky. Open your heart to the universe."

"I—I don't think I can physically do that," Jacob said.

Lavender's lip curled like she was ready to bark at him for making a joke during her class. The rumors about this woman's temper appeared to be spot on.

"So, you're saying that you're happy Lucia's gone?" I asked.

"Happy? No. Relieved. A little. I mean, it was only a matter of time before I lost my cool with her," Lavender said. "I guess you could say we had beef because of the 'name' thing, but mostly I was glad someone offed her before I did something bad."

"Like?"

Lavender became pensive. "I'm sure you heard about my prior, Gina. There's no point acting like you didn't. Everyone in Lake Basil knows about it. It was big news a couple of years ago."

"I had no idea," I said.

Jacob shook his head as well, though he'd been more focused on trying to execute the moves. We dropped into a strange position with both hands on the mat and then reached through to grab one ankle.

I caught sight of Lavender eyeing me. "Last time I lost my temper with a rude chick, I beat her within an inch of her life. Agg assault. They put me away for two years. But I'm out and I've changed my ways."

Jacob made an indistinct noise.

Lavender moved out of the complicated position, and I straightened, amazed by the fact that I'd made it through. "So, real talk?" Lavender stretched her neck left and right, swung her arms back and forth. "I'm glad she died before I did something dumb and ruined the good thing I've got going on here."

"Help." The plea had come from Jacob, who was still on all fours, one arm trapped beneath his chest and clasping his calf. "I think I'm stuck."

Nine

"CAN WE NEVER DO THAT AGAIN?" JACOB ASKED. "It's not for me."

"This is your fault for being so muscular," I said, as I brought him a bag of peas and pressed it to his lower back. "If you weren't such a gym bunny, you'd have been fine. You know, stretching is an integral part of a workout routine."

"Yeah, I forgot how you're a personal trainer." He winced as I shifted the peas carefully. "Ouch."

I pressed a kiss to his forehead. "I'm sorry, honey," I said. "I didn't realize it was going to be that intense. I shouldn't have involved you in my—" What could I call it? Curiosity? Sticking my nose where it didn't belong? My constant need to prove myself and that I was worth anything thanks to that small, mean voice that sounded an awful lot like my ex in my head.

If time was meant to heal all wounds, how come I still doubted myself like this?

"I wanted to come with you. Besides," Jacob said. "It was an adventure. Am I ever going to do it again? No. But if it will keep you away from that crazy woman, then—"

"Who, Lavender?"

"Careful," he said, "she might have followed us home and you know how she doesn't like her real name."

We sat in the living room with the view of Lake Basil. The tree where Lucia had "hidden" was empty, and a gust of wind disturbed the branches, sending a few leaves swirling toward the placid waters below.

I stroked Jacob's hair absently, staring out at it and pondering.

Lucia had been so intent on the recipe book and making her business work, that she had climbed that tree and later broken into the study. And then someone had murdered Lucia. Could it be as simple as it having been Lavender?

She fit the bill.

She was an angry woman with a prior charge. She'd hated Lucia, seemed openly relieved that she was dead, and had even said they had beef. But could it be that simple?

"—suspicious."

"Huh?" I had been so lost in my thoughts, I hadn't realized Jacob was talking.

"Just saying how that woman is suspicious. It's one thing to be open about disliking someone, another to be that angry about it," Jacob said. "Seems like she had a reason to want to get rid of Lucia."

"Maybe." I didn't add anything in.

Was it silly of me to want to keep Jacob out of this? He'd never had an issue with my curious streak before, but a part of me was afraid of relying on him in that way. What if he suddenly changed his mind and decided that I was *doing the wrong thing?*

Jacob frowned up at me. "You OK?"

"Sure," I said. "Just fine. Thinking about what's been going on, is all. And there's the restaurant. How on earth are you going to cook tonight after this?"

"I'll manage. Not my first run-in with yoga."

"Oh yeah?"

"Yeah, Brittany used to make Patrick and I do yoga, and get really irritated when we couldn't get the moves right." Jacob shook his head. "My brother has his flaws, but I'm glad that he's not married to her anymore." Jacob's brother had once been Brittany Brown's husband. She was single now and—

I blinked, catching movement out on the lake.

A boat sailed by, the person in it sitting pretty, paddles clutched in either hand. Speak of the she-devil, it was Brittany herself, driving the ends of those paddles into the water and speeding her way across the lake.

Since when did she row? Or do anything physically taxing that didn't involve handing out tongue-lashings from behind the counter at Cara's Coffee?

Jacob followed my line of sight and shook his head. He made to stand up, but groaned and sat back down again. "I think you might be right about me cooking tonight. We'll have to ask Ross to step in."

"No problem," I said. "You relax, and I'll handle it."

"You sure? I'm happy to chat with him—"

I stroked his hair again. "I've got it." It was going to be an interesting night at the restaurant without Jacob there but we'd manage. Besides, he'd need the rest, and I needed to think about what Lavender had told me.

Matilda stopped by the restaurant that evening before we opened, Jumbo, her gorgeous fluffy white Persian on the end of a cutesy pink leash. Jumbo meowed at me insistently until I picked him up and tucked him into my chest.

"How's Jacob holding up?" Matilda asked. "I can't believe he threw out his back doing yoga." She frowned. "Actually, I can believe that. Yoga isn't for babies. I mean, unless they're doing baby yoga, which I hear is a thing."

I laughed, thoroughly enjoying the chatter and Jumbo's insistence on rubbing the sides of his face against my chin. "Yes, pretty boy, I've missed you two. Yes, I have." The black cat that had been haunting Jacob's study hadn't returned, but I found myself looking out for him every night.

"Jacob," I said, "is cranky about not being able to cook. But the new sous chef has everything prepped and ready to go. He was a great choice."

"Better than Leo," Matilda said, then gestured for me to follow her off to one side, away from the reception area and closer to the bathrooms.

"What's up?" I asked, my fingers tangled in Jumbo's fur.

"I noticed something," Matilda said, "and I thought you should know about it."

"Sure, OK. What is it?"

"Remember how I have those cameras set up watching the street from my apartment." She pointed to her window above Dingle's Bakery across the street. The curtains were drawn, and the little black nub that was the camera lens was hidden from view, but I remembered it.

Jacob and I often teased Matilda about her people-watching habit.

"Sure."

"I noticed two people keep coming around the bakery. First one comes by in a fancy sports car and parks outside before driving off again," Matilda whispered. "Romeo Moretti."

I pursed my lips. Romeo.

What was he up to? If anyone would know who might have murdered Lucia, and what had happened to Uncle Rocco's recipe book, it was Moretti himself. I'd already decided I would pay him a visit—I was just working up the courage after our run-ins during summer. He wasn't the friendliest guy around.

"And the other one?" I asked. "Who else has been hanging around?"

"Leo, the sous chef," Matilda said. "I thought I should warn you, given what happened to the recipe book. And to Lucia."

"I appreciate it."

"Just be careful, Gina," Matilda said, taking Jumbo back from me. "There's something strange going on in town. It's not just the murder. I can feel it. Like there's... trouble on the horizon or something. That or I've had too much lavender tea."

Lavender tea. That only made me think of lavender and drew my mind back to the mystery at hand.

This wasn't going away on its own. The recipe book wouldn't find itself. And Detective Carter and the sheriff's department had been silent about the murder.

Matilda was right. Something was up.

I was going to figure out what it was.

$\mathcal{T}_{\varepsilon n}$

The following morning...

AFTER A QUICK COFFEE WITH JACOB, WHO WAS feeling a lot better after a good night's rest and a quick massage, I got into Jacob's car, grateful that he was happy to share it with me, and took the short drive out to the Moretti Mansion.

It wasn't that far removed from the lake itself, and the bumpy dirt roads that ran through this portion of town were both familiar and disconcerting today. The closer I drew to the mansion, the more I worried about returning to the scene of the crime.

I had no idea what to expect.

Sure, I could expect Romeo to absolutely lose it at my presence—the reason I'd tucked my pepper spray into my purse before leaving the house—but the rest of the Morettis were a mystery to me.

What about the patriarch of the family who I'd seen in those paintings inside the mansion? Who was he? Where was he?

Gravel crunched and turned under the wheels as I stopped in front of the gates to Moretti mansion, with their decorative letter "M"s made out of steelwork.

The front of the house was empty of cars for once, and the front doors were firmly shut. No police lines or seals. Whatever forensic work had been necessary, it was already complete, the scene released.

I leaned out of the driver's side window and hit the intercom button.

A click and then. "Hello?" A woman's voice, vaguely familiar.

"Hello, is Romeo Moretti around?" I asked.

"I'm afraid not," the woman said. "Romeo's gone into town."

"Are any of the Morettis around?"

A moment of fuzzy quiet. "Who's asking?"

"My name is Gina Romano," I said. "I wanted to talk to Romeo or any of the Morettis about what happened to Lucia. I was the one who found her body on the morning it happened, and I figured it would be important for us to talk." It sounded like a crock, even to my ears.

More fuzziness.

"Hello?"

"I'm opening the gates," the woman said.

I blinked my surprise. That was something at least. I hadn't expected to make it past the gates—I'd fully anticipated Romeo Moretti charging down toward me, a tire iron or baseball bat in hand. Recent events may have colored my perception, to be fair.

The gates clacked and swung inward, and a realization struck me.

These gates had been all the way open on the morning I'd arrived looking for the recipe book. So, Lucia must have let someone in? Or was it that she'd left them open after inviting her yoga instructor inside.

Lavender was still the most likely suspect after her confession about her prior. But why confess that if she was guilty? Unless it was to throw me off her scent.

After all, how could it be a coincidence that the day after the murder had taken place, she just happened to show up in the restaurant to have a meal. By herself.

I parked the car in front of the grand stone steps then got out, keenly aware of how out of place I was in front of this mansion. I wore sneakers, my hair tied back in a high ponytail, my blouse plain, and my jeans old and worn.

Funny, but not so long ago, I had been living the

corporate high society life in the City. Now, I felt as much a Lake Basilite as I did a City girl—more-so even.

One of those massive wooden doors creaked open, and an elderly woman appeared.

It was the housekeeper from the other day. The one who'd insisted she had to enter the house to clean.

She shuffled out a few steps, timid, but her uniform neat as a pin. "Mrs. Romano?"

"Miss," I said. "I remember you. You're—"

"Dolores. The housekeeper." She said it primly, but her gaze darted past me toward the entrance. "I can't invite you in. Mr. Moretti isn't home, and it wouldn't be appropriate."

Then why had she decided to let me in the gates at all?

"Romeo has gone to the restaurant," Dolores said, placing even emphasis on every word. She took my gaze and held it. "He wants to open it up again and make it a success."

"That's... OK. I wanted to talk to him about what happened to his sister," I said. "Lucia—"

"Lucia was a horrible woman," Dolores said, right away. "She treated me much like the rest of the family does. Like an extra. And I think it's true that the way you treat the help is a good indication of what kind of person you are. I—"

The gates clanked on the mechanism behind me, and I

turned. A black sleek SUV drove toward us, Romeo behind the wheel, his fingers be-ringed. He parked and flung the door open, hopping out onto the gravel.

"What's she doing in here, Dumbo?" Romeo asked.

Dolores stiffened. "My apologies, Romeo," she said, "but this woman asked to see you and—"

"And I don't want to see her, Dumbo," Romeo interrupted. "I wasn't here, so why are you letting her into our home?"

"I hadn't, sir."

"Listen, Dumbo—"

"Stop calling her that," I snapped.

Romeo cast a sidelong glance my way, sneering. "Yous think I give a darn about what you gotta say?"

"Romeo, your sister is dead and all you can do is stand here and mock your housekeeper. You should be—"

Romeo crossed the space between us rapidly, and my fingers flew to my purse, fumbling to open it and find the pepper spray inside. He squared up to me, his nose right in my face, his expensive cologne clingy and invasive. "You don't tell me what I am or what I gotta be, understand?" He pointed a thick finger at my face.

I narrowed my eyes at him. "And you get that finger out of my face before I break it."

Romeo growled low in his throat. He stepped back a pace and laughed, running a hand over his perfectly coiffed hair. "You trippin'," he said. "Now, get outta here before I call the cops." He strode past the housekeeper, whistling for her to follow him like she was a dog.

Dolores hesitated. She shuffled down the steps hurriedly then shoved a slip of paper toward me before rushing inside. The door shut with an ominous clang.

Eleven

Late that night...

JACOB AND I ARRIVED HOME WITH A PIZZA IN hand—made fresh in Romano's Family Restaurant—exhausted after a long day. Jacob's back was way better, but we had been absolutely swamped with customers today, and a full day spent moving around and on his feet hadn't done the injury any good.

He groaned as he got out of the car, circling to my side to open the door for me.

I tried to beat him to the punch, but I had the pizza in my lap and a lot on my mind. Namely, the note that Dolores, the Moretti's housekeeper, had given me this morning. I'd only given it the most cursory of glances because I'd had to be at the restaurant shortly after my "dismissal" by Romeo, and the note and its contents had consumed my thoughts ever since.

"Thank you," I said, hopping out of the car. "We should eat and get you to bed. Your back needs rest."

"I'm fine," Jacob grumbled, placing a fist in the small of his back and massaging it. "I got a little over excited today when the mayor came in for dinner."

I smiled at him. I had no idea what I'd done to deserve such a wonderful man. He cared about the restaurant, he worked hard, and he treated me with respect.

"You need rest," I said. "I'm in half a mind to call Ross and ask him to take over tomorrow no matter what you say."

"You wouldn't," Jacob replied. "Working in that restaurant is the only time I feel anything close to useful."

"Huh?" I unlocked the door for him since he was massaging with his knuckles, and we entered our home.

That had such a strange ring to it.

Our home.

The last time I'd shared a place with someone, it had been with my ex, and it had been an upscale apartment that had wound up cold and empty most of the time. Living with Jacob was so different to that—it was warm and cozy, even if the house was run down here or there. The guest bedroom needed work, the porch steps were soft and needed replacing.

"What did you mean by that, Jake?" I asked as we entered the kitchen and sat down at the table together. The pizza, a pepperoni tonight, smelled divine.

Jacob popped the lid, and we both grabbed slices. He leaned against the kitchen counter, chewing thoughtfully. "Nothing serious."

"Saying you don't feel useful is pretty serious."

"It's not that I don't feel useful," he said. "It's that you often won't let me be useful."

"That's just not true," I said. "You're the chef in my restaurant. How could I possibly—"

"Gina, come on."

"What?"

"Let's get real here," Jacob said, hoovering the last bit of his slice then washing his hands under the kitchen faucet.

"I am being real."

"Gina, you've been asking questions about Lucia for the last week and you haven't thought to talk to me about it. It's like you're still acting as if you're living with your aunt and uncle. You've probably talked to Sofia about the case more than you have to me."

I gnawed on the inside of my cheek, trying not to look guilty. Because he was right. I'd done my level best to keep Jacob out of this.

Because relying on him for help would mean accepting

that this was all real. That we were moving ahead, that we were living together, that this was more than just a passing *thing*. And sure, I should have accepted that all along—we were *living together*—but old habits died hard.

"Fine," Jacob said after a beat. "Suit yourself. Just do me a favor and don't go talking to Shawn Carter before you do to me."

"Shawn's the detective working the case," I said. "I have to talk to him if he wants to question me."

"Shawn likes you," Jacob said. "As in, 'likes you' likes you." He used inverted commas. "And he's going to do whatever it takes to get closer to you."

"That's—Well, that doesn't matter. I love you," I said.

Jacob nodded. "OK."

"What?"

"Nothing," he said. "Nothing. Just, uh, what's with the little note you've been sneaking peeks at all afternoon?"

Had I been that obvious? I'd thought I'd been so slick in the restaurant, hovering either at the bar or behind the hostess stand, checking out my fresh lead.

"It's just a slip of paper that I got from—" I broke off. It was a long story. And was it so wrong that I wanted this to myself? Just because we were living together, did that mean I had to share *everything* with Jacob? Surely, there could be a few things that I kept to myself?

"From?"

Irritation flared in my stomach.

Had things been simpler when I'd lived with Aunt Sofia and Uncle Rocco? I missed my nightly visits with Matilda and Jumbo. Living with Jacob was great, but what about the other parts of my life that were important to me.

The last time I had fallen in love with a man, I'd given up every facet of my personality for him, and I didn't want to do that again.

"It was a note from Dolores, the housekeeper at the Moretti's. I stopped by there today, hoping to talk to Romeo." Who did I want to be in this situation? The girlfriend who was honest? The one who was independent? Was there a middle-ground?

"Ah," Jacob said. "What did she say?"

"That she thinks Romeo did it. That she's scared of him," I said.

"Interesting," Jacob replied.

"Why's that?"

"Because after we took that back-breaking yoga session," Jacob said, "I started doing a little research of my own about Lavender McGee. Turns out, the woman that she attacked?"

"Yeah?"

"That was Dolores Bridges. The Moretti's housekeeper." Jacob wore a self-satisfied expression. "I thought that might be relevant."

"And you were going to tell me this, when?" I asked.

"When you finally decided I was worth talking to about this kind of thing again," Jacob said. "Now, I'm going to head up to bed." He pressed a kiss to my cheek on the way out of the kitchen, and I stood there until his footsteps had faded on the stairs.

What was wrong with me? Why was I frustrated about the fact that he'd given me a valuable piece of information?

The fact was, Jacob was trying to help, and I was getting upset about it. It was silly.

But I couldn't shake that bone deep irritation no matter how hard I tried.

Twelve

THE FOLLOWING MORNING, I SAT OUT IN THE backyard with its view of the pristine lake, the last of the heat from summer present only in the sun washing my back. I shrugged my coat higher, wrapping it around myself and took a long drink of strong coffee.

Jacob had gone out to have brunch with his brother, who was in town for business, and had left me at the house to contemplate my navel and the case. The two were not mutually exclusive.

This morning's coffee had been just the same as any other since we'd moved in together, with Jacob pleasant and loving as always. Which, of course, made me feel like an even bigger meanie for my frustrations the night before.

I had sort of pinpointed why I was irritated, but it was a selfish reason, and that made things even worse.

I wanted the case for myself. After deciding that I would share my life with Jacob, after being with him at the restaurant all day long, and now at home with him too, I wanted this last little piece of *something* just for me.

Which was either toxic or reasonable, and I couldn't decide which.

I fished my phone out of my pocket, fully intent on calling Matilda and asking for advice. She'd been through a tricky relationship in the past, and she'd know whether I was being unreasonable or not.

Before I could hit the button to call her, a voice traveled across the lake toward me.

I frowned, searching for whoever had talked.

Nothing and nobody.

It had to be somebody across the lake, right? Voices traveled over water. I checked that there was no one in the tree anyway, and my skin prickled at the memory of Lucia up there. Lucia who was now gone.

Another bout of laughter.

A boat drifted into view, and I froze in place, watching it.

Two women were aboard the boat. One of them was unmistakable—Lavender McGee, complete with bright purple workout clothing and rusty red hair, doing a headstand—and the other was the spawn of evil herself, Brittany Brown.

Brittany was doing her best attempt at the same yoga pose Lavender had put us in during couples yoga.

"You've got to be kidding me," Brittany said, totally unaware of how her voice traveled across the water. They weren't even that far out. "Like, that's not a thing, is it?"

"Totally is a thing," Lavender said. "And you know what else? Lucia complained about him nonstop. They were beefing, for sure. She said that if she ever saw him around the restaurant again, she was going to fire him for what he did."

"I can't say I blame her," Brittany replied. "Like, going out to the main competitor like that? I would've fired him, like, yesterday."

"You can't blame Leo, though." Lavender came out of the headstand without rocking the boat, which was impressive. "Lucia was an ugly person."

"Ugly," Brittany agreed. "She liked to gossip about people all the time. And she called people names. Like, real character-breaking stuff."

This was a severe degree of hypocrisy coming from Brittany, who had nicknamed me "Pizzaface Romano" during high school, and used that as my given name whenever she saw me.

"Yeah, well, that's why she's dead. When you act like that, it's bound to happen to you." Lavender made a choking noise to mimic Lucia's death, and Brittany didn't say anything.

The boat drifted on, the women trying different poses, until Lavender spotted me sitting at the table behind Jacob's cabin.

"Who's that?" she asked, raising a hand to her brow to spy on me, blissfully unaware that I could hear every single word of their conversation.

Brittany swiveled in the boat a little too quickly, and it rocked from side-to-side. "Oh, that's just Pizzaface. She lives out here now because she's such a nuisance to societ — Whoa!"

"Stop moving, Brit," Lavender said. "Stop."

But Brittany couldn't help herself. The more the boat rocked, the more she tried to steady herself, until she was caught in a vicious cycle of rocking and steadying, stomping one foot and then the other in a desperate bid for purchase.

"What are you—?"

Brittany let out a squeal as her feet slipped out from underneath her. She toppled over backward and the boat tipped both women into the water with two fantastic splashes.

I rose from my chair, but there wasn't much I could do, and by the time I'd taken a couple of steps, both of the women had resurfaced and were spluttering. Lavender cast furious curses at Brittany who looked suitably sheepish.

They seemed to have control over their boat, so I grabbed my coffee mug and headed into the house, inhaling the scent of wood and a light hint of basil from the pesto Jacob had whipped up early this morning to store in our fridge.

I grabbed my tablet from the study and sat down in the chair, my gaze traveling toward the bookshelf that was still missing my uncle's recipe book.

"Wrong," I muttered. "This is all wrong."

And then I opened a fresh memo on the tablet and started typing.

To-Do List:

- *Figure out who took the recipe book and where it could be. Retrieve it. Best place to start would be at the Moretti mansion, but how to get in there? Talk to Dolores?*
- *Find out why Dolores thinks Romeo's the one who did it. Would Romeo kill his own sister?*
- *How are Lavender and Dolores connected? Was Lavender the last one seen with Lucia or does she have an alibi?*
- *How to get the alibis? Not like they'll just outright tell me where they were. I'm not a cop.*

- *Talk to Leo again. Matilda mentioned that she saw both Romeo and Leo hanging around outside the restaurant.*

And now that I'd literally heard Lavender talking about how Lucia had complained about her chef, that was more reason to suspect him.

I was convinced that Lucia had been the one to take the recipe book, but my gut told me there was more to this than I'd initially thought.

Could the killer have wanted the recipe book? Or was there another reason for Lucia's untimely demise?

I needed to talk to Matilda about this. Not only would she have the camera recordings, but she might have some insight.

Thirteen

"Did you run it past Jacob?" Matilda asked the exact question I didn't need to hear.

She'd ducked upstairs to her apartment, Jumbo trotting ahead of her with his white tail poker straight and quivering with excitement at the potential for a mid-morning snack, so that we could chat. Her bakery bustled with activity, especially now that the cooler months were upon us.

Lake Basilites loved a good cupcake and now, thanks to my best friend, they loved a good cup of tea. Many of them would joke around and try to "do a British accent" when they said "cup of tea." It always made Matilda smile, because she'd had a grandmother from the U.K., and me cringe because they were butchering the accent.

I shifted on Matilda's sofa, trying to settle myself so that I wouldn't squirm too much under her scrutiny.

Matilda was a few years older than me but wiser than I'd ever be, and she gave me that fixed stare that pierced right through my center. It was like she could see through all my nonsense and cut right to the truth.

"What's going on?" Matilda asked from her favorite armchair. Jumbo had jumped into her lap, and he purred and rubbed against her palm.

Suddenly, the apartment wasn't "pleasantly warm" after the cold outside, but sweltering. What was with the third degree questioning? "Nothing. I just wanted to talk about the case and what I'd discovered so far. You know, about Lucia and the murder. And the recipe book."

"Uh-huh. And you didn't talk to Jacob about this, why?"

"I always talk to you," I said. "And who says I didn't talk to Jacob?"

"The guilty look on your face, for one. You reacted pretty strongly when I suggested it. I mean, it's not like he's going to be mad about you poking around, right? So what's the big deal?"

"There's no big deal," I said. "I guess I like having something for myself. It's nice to be independent."

Matilda gave me a knowing look.

"Don't."

"I'm just saying," Matilda said, "that if you wanted to be independent, you could have stayed single. Usually partners share things with each other. That's how it used to be when I was in a relationship, anyway. When dinosaurs roamed the earth."

I rolled my eyes at her. "Look, I'll figure it out, but right now, I need to talk to my friend about my thoughts and get her opinion."

"I'll check if she's around." Matilda made a show of looking around, and Jumbo placed a white paw on her chin out of frustration at the lack of petting.

"Very funny," I said. "But I'm serious."

"All right. Lay it on me." Matilda had been through it in Lake Basil too. I'd shared the details about previous murder mysteries with her, so she was sort of used to it by now. She paled when I talked about Lucia's death, though.

"So, you see, I can't figure out how it fits together. Nobody *really* wants to talk to me. The recipe book is still missing, and I can't place my finger on what's going on."

Matilda wriggled her nose from left to right. "Well, it could be any of them. But Lavender sounds particularly suspicious, what with her anger issues and all. And then there's the fact that Romeo's just not a nice guy. Remember when he banged on his chest like he was King Kong and had a fight with the customers in Moretti's Italian?"

"How could I forget?"

"And I have noticed him slowing down and stopping outside your restaurant a lot lately."

"You mentioned that," I said. "Can I see what you mean?"

"Sure." Matilda got up and grabbed her laptop. She brought it over and plopped down next to me, putting her feet up on her coffee table. "Leo stopped. He came by a few times, but I think that was because you interviewed him to be a sous chef, right?"

"Right. I had to let him down because he wasn't a match."

Matilda pulled a face. "I can imagine he wouldn't be. I ate at Moretti's just to try it out and—"

I affected a scandalized expression. "You cheated on Romano's?"

Matilda stuck out her tongue. "As I was saying, I ate there once, and the food was terrible. Burned garlic and… just bad. I don't know if that was because of Lucia's ownership or just because the chef was so darn bad." She navigated toward the files on her laptop and double-tapped the pad to open one. "Here, see. That's Romeo's car."

And indeed, a fancy car drove by the restaurant on screen. That by itself wouldn't have been noteworthy, but it was also the fact that the timestamp said he'd come around closing time for Romano's. After his sister's murder.

Why?

"How many times did he do this?" I asked.

Matilda fast forwarded through the footage so I could witness it for myself. "Look," she said. "There's the second time. And the third."

My eyes widened. This was truly alarming.

Romeo had circled the restaurant not once or twice, but a total of seven times before he'd left. And on the last time, he'd parked down the street and waited for us to leave.

Was he following us? Following Jacob and me? But why?

"Creepy," I said. "Do you think we should go to Shawn about this?"

"I mean, yeah. It seems important."

I was hesitant. The last time I'd talked to Shawn about Romeo Moretti, I'd accused Romeo of having trashed my car. But I'd been wrong. Just as wrong as I'd been about Romeo being a murderer.

What if I was wrong this time and there was a simple explanation for this behavior?

It could be that Romeo was concerned for our safety? I dismissed the thought immediately. It was even more ridiculous than my accusations had been the last time.

"When did he start doing this?" I asked. "Do you know?"

"Well, honestly, I only checked recently and my cloud only stores up to a week prior. So, I don't have anything from around the time of the murder, unfortunately."

"Darn." That would have gone a great way to either clearing or pointing us toward Romeo. If he'd been around the restaurant around the time of the murder, he couldn't have killed his sister.

"Look at this," Matilda said, pointing at the screen.

I leaned in. "What?"

"Look at the car carefully when it drives by."

I did exactly as she'd said.

"See there?" Matilda fingered the screen as the car made another turn around the restaurant. "Do you see them?"

"Yeah. Shadows. There's more than one person in the car," I said.

But who? And why were they watching the restaurant?

Fourteen

That evening...

Romano's was as busy as always, bustling with activity. Violet and Charles moved around the interior of the restaurant, stopping at tables, covered in white tablecloths, accented with silverware and gorgeous crystal glasses, to take orders. Despite the finery, Romano's had a friendly atmosphere—a coziness that said you could bring your family here for pasta and pizza, antipasti and dessert. The vanilla ice cream drops were exquisite.

We hadn't had a complaint all night, and that was partly because most of the tourists had left Lake Basil's shores by now, and the locals had taken back the night.

I manned the hostess station near the front doors,

occasionally answering a call and confirming that we were fully booked.

Delicious dishes streamed out of the kitchen, from the ravioli to the farfalle, to the fusilli. The fact that the recipe had come from Uncle Rocco's book was wedged in my mind, that it was missing was a constant irritant.

If only I could figure it out!

I'd been through so much in Lake Basil, surely a recipe book wouldn't elude me. If I could just—

My phone buzzed on the desk, and I lifted it, frowning at the notification from a hidden number. I had a voice message, and a missed call.

Nobody needed my assistance, both Vi and Charles were preoccupied with their tables, and the bar was hopping, so I listened to the message.

A voice whispered through the speaker, sending a shiver down my spine. "If you want to get into the Moretti's house, you'll find the door in the western wing unlocked. It will be unlocked until midnight. You'll find what you're looking for in the kitchen."

I whipped the phone away from my ear and stared at it then stabbed a button to replay the message.

I listened to it a second time, trying to place the soft voice. It was feminine, but that didn't mean much. Anyone could put on a voice. And why was the owner of this particular voice trying to encourage me to head over to the Moretti mansion?

And to do what? To find what I'm looking for?

The recipe book.

They had to be talking about the recipe book.

The front door of Romano's opened and my aunt and uncle entered, arm-in-arm. My uncle was looking healthier than he had in years, possibly because my aunt had been crushing his multi-vitamins into his Sunday minestrone, and he gave me a broad grin.

"Gina!" I circled the hostess stand, trying to put the strange message out of my mind for now.

"Uncle Rocco." I gave him a hug, and he squeezed me tight, burying me in his familiar smell. It reminded me of home—a mixture of old spice and pizza dough. I wasn't sure if it was just an association my brain made with Uncle Rocco or if he'd made pizza dough recently, but it was a nice smell.

Aunt Sofia hugged me next, pinching my cheek and telling me how proud she was of me.

Whenever Uncle Rocco dropped by the restaurant, he would swell up at the sight of it bustling with activity and happy customers. When he'd fallen ill, not too long ago, the place had nearly fallen apart. Now, he was an investor —because I'd forced him to be, rather than giving me the place entirely—and proud of it.

I guided them over to the best table in the house, specifically reserved for them, and sat them down.

"Good morning, Uncle, Auntie." Violet had arrived to take their orders. Everyone who worked at Romano's knew them as Aunt and Uncle. Or in Vi's case, Auntie. "What can I get for you this evening?"

"A glass of white wine," Aunt Sofia said, pink-cheeked and excited. "It's not every day we come out for dinner."

"You'd swear I never treat you, Sof," my uncle said, as he perused the menu like he hadn't been here a million times before. Or like we didn't use several of his recipes. "I'll take a tall, cold glass of beer."

"Now, Rocky, you know that's not the healthiest—"

"If you can have wine, I can have my beer, woman," my uncle blustered. "Now, how are things looking around here, Gina?"

"Great, Uncle, why do you ask?"

"We parked down the street," Aunt Sofia whispered, conspiratorially. "We had to walk all the way here, and on the way, we passed Moretti's Italian Restaurant."

Uncle Rocco looked like he wanted to spit at the mention of the place.

"Oh yeah? They're closed, aren't they?"

"Not anymore," Uncle Rocco said. "Apparently, they opened tonight. I saw that clown Romeo Moretti standing in the middle of the place, talking to his staff. It's a miracle anyone decided to show up for work there after what that family's put them through."

"They've been very cruel to their staff," Aunt Sofia said. "That's the rumor, anyway. I sure wouldn't want to work there."

"As if I'd let you work in another restaurant," Uncle Rocco said.

Aunt Sof reached across the table and squeezed his hand. Uncle Rocco always got prideful when he visited Romano's, but I didn't blame him. He'd built this restaurant with his bare hands. He'd put in the years of blood, sweat, and tears. Even when it had been a pizzeria, back when I'd been a little girl, it had been the most popular place to eat in Lake Basil.

"You're sure they opened up again?" I asked. "For real?"

"Oh yeah," Uncle Rocco said. "They're open all right. And Romeo's manning the front of the house, looking like he's ready to run the place into the ground."

I grimaced.

But that meant that the caller, whoever they were, had to be well informed. I had a hunch about who it was—Dolores, the housekeeper—but I couldn't be entirely sure.

"Thanks for letting me know, Uncle," I said, "but I've got everything under control."

"I bet you do, honey." Aunt Sofia beamed up at me.

Violet returned with their drinks in no time and stood taking their order while I returned to the hostess stand to usher in another group of diners. They had a reservation as well. I glanced out the window and spotted a man standing across the street, right outside Dingle's Bakery's glass front door.

His face was in shadow, and he wore a suit and tie.

Before I could rush out to see who it was, he turned and walked off down the street, leaving me with an ominous feeling. Something weird was happening in Lake Basil. I wasn't sure if the Morettis had started it, or if this was all because of Lucia's murder, but I had to find out what it was before things got any worse.

The minute I had my chance, I'd take it. I had to find out what was waiting for me in the kitchen at the Moretti mansion.

Fifteen

IN RETROSPECT, THIS MIGHT NOT HAVE BEEN THE best idea. I had arrived at the Moretti mansion's front gates to find them standing ajar and several cars parked out front. Lucia's vehicle wasn't among them, and Romeo's SUV was gone, but there were others.

Many others.

And the front doors of the mansion had been thrown open. People moved in and out of them, talking, eating canapes, and wearing black to the soundtrack of a thumping house song that didn't suit the mood they were going for.

A wake. This was a wake. Or a memorial service.

But what kind of people hosted a midnight memorial service? And played house music at said service? And treated it as more of a party than a memorial?

Regardless, the gates of the mansion had been left wide to admit arriving guests, even though the party was in full swing.

I crept onto the gravel driveway and into the bushes that ran along the stone walls enclosing the Moretti grounds.

Through the leaves, I barely made out the front of the house, the grand hallway beyond with its tacky gold and red color-scheme. People milled around, and I caught glimpses of them and the massive picture that had been erected in front of the grand staircase—a blown up image of Lucia Moretti, wearing her hair in a pouf.

Bizarre. This whole thing is bizarre.

And it was clearly a trap.

The last time I'd gone adventuring in hedges or bushes on someone else's property—a mansion too, by chance— I'd wound up nearly dead, covered in nettle stings, and half-delirious. But that was more because of the lack of sleep than the bushes.

Regardless, this was a bad idea.

And I was going to continue making it if it meant I'd find out the truth.

I moved through the bushes, keeping to the darkness and watching the house like a hawk. If any of the party-goers so much as glanced in my direction, I'd duck down and hope to heck they hadn't seen me. A great plan. One of my finest.

I reached the side of the house or "the west wing" as the mysterious voice message had called it, and stopped, eyeing the side door to the house. It was quieter this side, but the thump of music was audible.

My throat tightened at the thought of darting across the grass toward the side doors—French doors with panes of glass that viewed a dim hallway.

Three, two, one, g—

A figure rounded the corner, stumbling into view. They halted and sighed, drawing a phone out of their pocket.

"Salvatore!" A woman shouted from the side of the house, and a second figure emerged from the shadows. "Salvatore, what are you doing?"

"Keep it down, would you?" The man's voice was husky and deep. "We're not meant to be out here."

"Would you relax?" the woman purred. "Nobody can hear us. Your wife's too busy partying to care about where you are."

Intrigue spiked in my chest. An illicit affair at a memorial service? This was gossip-worthy, or would have been in my aunt's eyes, but it might not have anything to do with Lucia or the recipe book.

"Get your hands off me," Salvatore said, in that gruff, gravelly voice. "I'm the head of this household. I can't afford to be seen with you. I've warned you about this—"

"I know that," she said. "But I—I want to comfort you, Salvatore. Your daughter is gone."

"You keep your mouth shut. You don't know what you're talking about. You didn't know Lucia." And then Salvatore strode away from the woman and around the front of the house. The mistress—I assumed she had to be given the conversation—hesitated then let out a huff of air and followed Salvatore moments later.

Salvatore had to be the surly man I'd seen in the pictures in the mansion. The man who had clearly been the patriarch of the family, who was somewhat of a mystery. I'd never heard a single rumor about him, which was saying a lot given my closeness with Aunt Sofia.

I waited a few heartbeats then started across the grass, walking powerfully rather than running. I figured that if anyone came around the side of the house and saw me, they'd think I was another guest. Even if I was wearing jeans and a peacoat.

As promised, the side doors were unlocked, and I slipped into the interior of the house.

I moved through it, my heart pounding as I sidled down the darkened hall.

There was a light on further down, and I peered through an open archway and into a glistening kitchen.

This was it. This was the place.

I scanned the kitchen, but nothing seemed out of place. There was no package waiting for me or an obvious item that could have been a clue.

Tentatively, I entered the kitchen—marble flooring, a kitchen island with copper pots and pans hanging overhead—and continued my search.

Nothing.

Where was the mystery item that this voice message had promised me? Unless this had all been a trap.

My gaze rested on the block of knives, and my heart turned over. They all had the exact same hilt as the one that had been used to murder Lucia. That decorative "M" lettering scrawled on silver and that had to mean that it had come from here.

Hadn't it?

Except none of the knives were missing, and just where was—?

"What do you mean?" Romeo Moretti's voice echoed through the house. "In the kitchen?" Footsteps tapped in the hall, and I froze for a millisecond before diving out of sight and pressing my back against the kitchen island.

Moments later, Romeo strode into the kitchen, talking on his phone.

My instincts had been right. Someone had set me up for a trap in the Moretti mansion, knowing very well that I would come to find the truth.

And now, *I* was the one seconds away from being discovered.

Sixteen

ROMEO MORETTI'S COLOGNE WAS SO THICK IT tickled my nose, and I placed a hand over my face to keep from sneezing.

He was on the other side of the kitchen island, his steps painfully loud in my ears—the heels of his dress shoes tapping on the sparkling tiles. "There's no one here," he said. "I don't know what you're talking about, but I'm tired of your games. So, I suggest you—"

Romeo rounded the kitchen island and spotted me crouched down like a little gremlin beside it. He let out a shout and dropped his phone.

I darted toward the exit, running around the kitchen island and toward the hall, but Romeo quickly moved to block my path. There was no choice but to run toward the entrance of the house—the grand foyer and staircase where everyone was partying and wearing black.

Romeo growled low in his throat. "You," he said. "I knew you were—"

I didn't give him a chance to talk. Instead, I spun on my heel and sprinted out into the hall.

"Hey! Get back here!" Romeo's shout followed me, but the tail-end was lost in the house music that thumped through the mansion. People, dressed in black, many of their clothes expensive, jumped out of my way, splashing drinks here or there.

Shocked cries from faces I didn't recognize. Faces that didn't belong in Lake Basil or weren't local to this area.

Who were these people in their stark black suits, their cotton t-shirts, their ties and expensive dresses?

I sprinted past waiters with trays, trying my best not to knock into anyone or anything, the shouts behind me telling me that Romeo was on the chase.

If it had been just us two, I would have pepper-sprayed the dude and been done with it, but there were too many factors here.

Panic threaded through my veins, forcing me onward, and I burst out of the mansion and nearly tumbled down the stairs in my haste to be gone. I sprinted down the drive-way, kicking up gravel, grateful for my sensible sneakers.

"Get back here!" Romeo cried, but he sounded further away.

The mansion gates started closing up ahead, and I put on a final burst of speed, my lungs burning. I slipped between the gates just in time. They shut behind me, and I spun around looking back up at the house.

Romeo stood on the front steps in the distance, glaring, his phone in hand.

Now wasn't the time to stick around, so I got into Jacob's car and started it, taking the road back toward the restaurant.

I'd barely made it a block when police lights flashed behind the car. I pulled over to the clipped whoop of a siren.

Shawn Carter emerged from the squad car parked behind me, and I groaned.

Great. What now?

Had Romeo called him and reported me?

Shawn sauntered up to the driver's side of the vehicle, and I rolled the window down, my license and the registration already clasped in my clammy palm. "Hi Shawn," I said. "Why are you out tonight?" He was a detective. It wasn't like it was his job to patrol. Granted, this was a small town and our police station serviced the entire county, but still.

"Gina," Shawn said, with a long-suffering sigh. He

leaned an arm on the car door, giving me a hard stare. He wasn't a bad-looking man, but right about now, he had "mean" written all over his face. "What have you been up to?"

"I was just driving back to the restaurant to pick up Jacob," I said.

I'd darted out before closing so that I would be back in time to pick him up. The message had said before midnight, and that had been my only window of opportunity—the kitchen closed at 10:45 p.m., and the staff would be cleaning up until 11:30 p.m..

"That's good to know," Shawn said, with a hint of sarcasm, "but you didn't answer my question. What are you doing out here?"

"I was taking a drive," I said. "And what are *you* doing out here, Shawn? I thought you'd be more focused on Lucia's murder."

Shawn gave me a wry smile. "Funny, Gina, because that's exactly what I'm doing out here."

"That's good. Then you probably want to get back to—"

"You've gotta be kidding me with this, Romano." Shawn's tone was gruff. "You know, the Morettis are trouble but you come out here, anyway? Real talk? You got some kind of death wish to be acting the way you do."

"Shawn!"

"I'm serious. They're—Well, it doesn't matter what they are, but you should be staying away from them, not coming out here to crash their parties," Shawn said.

So Romeo *had* called him about our interlude. Our useless interlude, as whoever had left me the message had blatantly lied about their being anything of interest in the kitchen.

"You're lucky I'm a patient man," Shawn said. "And you're lucky that Romeo Moretti and Salvatore Moretti don't want to press charges."

"For what? I didn't do anything."

"Trespassing," Shawn said. "That's a thing, you know, Gina. You know what else is a thing?" He waited for me to ask, but I kept my mouth shut—believe it or not, I knew when that was the better option. "Interfering in an ongoing investigation is a thing. Obstructing a police investigation is a thing."

"I don't know what you're talking about, Shawn."

He gave me a hard, unwavering stare and kept his silence, leaning on the car door, the scent of him drifting through the interior.

I kept my peace, even though I had the distinct urge to just open up and tell him everything. About the message, the recipe book, the confusion about Lavender and Romeo, about Leo and Dolores. But if I told him anything, that would be admitting that I'd been out there tonight.

And so far, every time I'd tried to talk to Shawn about a case, he'd been resistant. Or he had since he'd confessed his feelings to me and I hadn't returned them.

"Fine, Gina," he said. "Don't say nothing, but I know what's really going on here."

"So, can I go?" I asked.

"Yeah." Shawn nodded. "Sure, you can go. But I'm going to follow you back to the restaurant so that I know you're not getting into any trouble."

"That's not necessary," I said.

"Oh, but it is." And then he walked back to his squad car and got inside, waiting for me to drive off.

He couldn't be serious, could he? I started the engine and drove off down the road, my nerves shot and gaze darting to Shawn's lights in my rearview mirror. Detective Carter started the car and followed me all the way back to Romano's.

Seventeen

This was beyond embarrassing.

Not only had Shawn followed me back to Romano's Family Restaurant, but he had parked outside of it, right behind Jacob's car, and walked me up to the door. Or rather, he'd followed me while I'd stormed toward it.

The interior was empty except for Jacob, who sat at a central table on his phone, concern creasing his brow. I hadn't even thought to check my phone once before I'd driven off from the Morettis, and guilt swam through me.

It was nothing compared to the anger at Shawn for following me back to the restaurant, however.

"Can you just leave me alone, please?" I turned around, glaring at Shawn. I didn't want to go into the restaurant and tell Jacob about what had happened with Shawn nearby.

"Nope," he said. "I want to ensure that you don't do anything rash, even if that means following you two lovebirds back to your love shack."

"I'm sure there's a better use for your time, Shawn. And isn't that stalking?"

Before he could answer, the door to Romano's clacked open and Jacob stepped out. "Gina? What's going on out here?"

"Nothing," I said mutinously. "Shawn was just leaving."

"Afraid I can't do that."

Jacob ran his fingers through his hair, spearing the detective with a glare. He didn't like Shawn under the best of circumstances, and this certainly wasn't them. Movement caught my eye from across the street, and I spotted Matilda and Jumbo watching from their apartment above the bakery.

What I would have done to be up there rather than down here right now.

"What's going on?" Jacob repeated stiffly.

I didn't want to say a word. I couldn't say anything without implicating myself and confirming that I had been out at the Moretti's place tonight.

"Your girl decided it would be a good idea to drive out to the Moretti mansion and crash Lucia's memorial service," Shawn said, adjusting the belt that looped through his jeans. "Got a call from Romeo Moretti. He was pretty darn angry about the fact that she gatecrashed their event."

I didn't say anything, but white hot anger flooded my veins.

Shawn was right. I had done all of those things. But the way he said it made me sound like a madwoman. Like I'd been completely irrational.

Where the truth was, I'd only been *partly* irrational.

I *had* received that mysterious message that had led me there. But I couldn't tell Jacob that in front of Shawn.

"Gina, is this true?" Jacob asked.

I didn't say anything.

"She's been quiet ever since I found her driving out near the Moretti's place," Shawn said, then jerked a thumb over his shoulder toward Jacob's car. "I assume that's your vehicle."

"Yeah."

Shawn nodded. "Maybe next time, you shouldn't lend out your car to a woman who—"

"I'd stop right there if I were you," Jacob said, raising a hand. "You can say whatever you want about me, Carter, but you don't say anything about Gina. Got it?"

"Or what, Murphy? What are you going to do?"

A thick tension hung in the air.

Jacob couldn't threaten Shawn without making things much worse and Shawn knew that. He relished it, in fact. Was this his cruel punishment for my rejection of him? This was so targeted. I doubt he would have followed any other resident of Lake Basil back to their home if they'd broken the rules.

No, he would have straight up arrested them.

"Or I'll handle it and you," Jacob said, taking a step forward, squaring his shoulders and looking down on the detective. He was taller. Shawn was stockier.

"Handle me? That a threat?" Shawn gave a chuckle. "Man, I hope it's a threat."

Jacob opened his mouth, but I pressed a hand over his arm and squeezed. "Enough," I said. "Jake, let's just go home. Please. Let's lock up and go home. We can talk in the car."

Jacob was white-lipped with rage, but he let out a breath, shook his head and stepped away from Shawn. "Fine." But he let his gaze linger on Shawn in a silent warning.

I locked up the restaurant hurriedly, and we got back into Jacob's car. He took the wheel, while I sat on the edge of the passenger seat, the seat belt digging into my collar bone.

Shawn's squad car tailed us all the way back to the house and only drove off after we'd gone inside.

"I'm going to report him," Jacob said, anger making his words tight.

"Jake, this is my fault."

"What happened out there? Why did you go to the Moretti's place?"

I bit down on my bottom lip. "I was following a lead. I thought I was going to find the recipe book, but it turned out it was a dead end. Romeo Moretti caught me snooping around and—well, you know the rest."

Jacob stood staring at me in silence.

"Jake?"

"I can't believe this," he grunted, ruffling his dark hair again. "I can't believe that you—Look, Gina, I get it, you don't want my help. You don't want me involved in your life, which is, it's just bizarre since we're living together now, but can you just—Just do me a favor and not use my car when you're committing crimes?"

"Jake, I wasn't—"

"Trespassing and breaking and entering are both crimes, Gina, last I checked," Jacob said, walking toward the base of the stairs. He flicked on the hall light, casting the frustration in his expression into sharp relief. "I don't know if I'm not worthy of being a part of your investigations or whatever or if you don't trust me, but do me a favor and don't endanger our life together by doing things like this."

"I wasn't trying to—"

"It doesn't matter what you were trying to do. You're keeping secrets."

I exhaled sharply. "Am I not allowed to have things that are my own? Just for me? I'm sorry, but I'm just not used to having to share everything about my life with—"

"Then you shouldn't have said yes to moving in with me. I'm not saying we have to be on top of each other. I'm not even saying you have to tell me everything. I'm asking that you don't endanger your life in my car. Is that too much to ask? You can't want to be independent from me and then use the—" He cut off, letting out a breath. "I'm angry. I don't want to lose my temper at you right now, so I'm going to dip out." He walked to the front door and grabbed the keys.

"Jake, wait."

"I'll be home later," he said. "Just—Just don't do anything dangerous while I'm gone." And then he exited our house and shut the door with a curt snap.

Eighteen

The following morning...

JACOB HADN'T COME HOME UNTIL THE EARLY
hours of the morning. I sat at the kitchen table, clasping a
mug of coffee between my palms, contemplating what I
had done and how he felt about it. He was right.

A part of me was holding onto how my ex had made
me feel. I had committed everything to him, only to have
him be the one keeping secrets from me. A mistress.

Keeping my secrets from Jacob wasn't fair either, even
if they were related to cases and mysteries rather than clan-
destine relationships.

I hadn't slept a wink last night, not until he'd come
home, and even then he had been unwilling to talk. This

was my fault, and I had to handle this carefully because I couldn't stand the thought of losing Jacob.

Footsteps creaked on the stairs, and I straightened, peering around at Jacob as he entered the kitchen. He gave me a bleary-eyed glance before heading over to the coffee pot in the corner.

"Jake," I said, clearing my throat. "Jake, I'm sorry. You were right. I shouldn't have kept where I was going from you, especially since it was dangerous."

He shook his head, his back to me. "I don't want you to say anything that you don't mean, Gina. The truth is, I want you to have your independence. I don't want to be controlling. Relationships are about compromise."

"They're also about communication," I said, "and I've done a poor job of that. So, really, I *am* sorry, and I'm going to be better at it."

Jacob came over and sat down at the table with me. He placed his hand on mine, brushing his fingers over the backs of my knuckles, and I relaxed. "Look, you don't have to share every facet of your life with me. I'm happy with what we have."

"Thank you for saying that," I said, "but I was being stubborn. I guess I was just worried you'd try to stop me from doing all the silly things I do when I'm chasing down leads. Even though I shouldn't be chasing down anything. It's not like I'm a cop."

"You should have been." Jacob laughed, taking a sip of his coffee. "You do a better job of it than Carter does."

"Don't let him hear you say that," I said.

"I don't care what he hears me say." Jacob's expression darkened. "The man doesn't know his place. What kind of stunt was that? Following us home. It's ridiculous."

I didn't say anything.

I was grateful that we'd been able to resolve our issue, even if it could have been prevented with better communication on my part.

"So," Jacob said, "do you want to chat about what happened out there last night? At the Moretti's place? Or would you prefer to keep that kind of stuff as just your thing?" It was sweet that he was asking rather than just trying to get me to tell him, straight up.

"I'm happy to talk about it," I said, letting go of that fear that I would lose myself by sharing this with him. I had to let it go if I wanted to stop acting like a loon and endangering our relationship. Jacob was a good man. He deserved honesty.

"So what happened?"

I broke it down for him briefly then brought out my phone and played the message for him. Now that I was out of the restaurant, the voice didn't sound as feminine. "What do you think?" I asked.

Jacob brushed his fingers over his creased brow. "I

think... Huh. Usually I would tell you to take something like this to the cops, but since Shawn is being, well, Shawn, I guess that's out of the question."

"I don't get who would have done this. It has to be the killer, right? They must know that I'm invested in what's happening with the case. They wanted to lead me on a wild goose chase."

"I'd say they succeeded in leading you on a wild goose chase," Jacob said. "But that voice... It sounds familiar. I can't place it, though."

"Pity. I'm going to have to figure out what's going on sooner or later. I'm no closer to finding the recipe book or the murderer," I said. "And it creeps me out knowing that there's some knife-wielding psycho on the loose." That reminded me of the knives in the Moretti's kitchen. It seemed like the murder weapon had to have come from there, right? Especially since the hilts had been engraved with the letter "M."

Jacob and I pondered the case for a little longer, but neither of us had anything new to bring to the table. Lavender was suspicious and didn't have an alibi. Leo was too. Dolores seemed like she'd wanted to talk, and I'd been sure that she'd left me the message, but nothing had come of my visit to the Moretti Mansion except for a headache. And then there was Romeo himself.

Was it possible that Romeo had finally tired of his

sister and gotten rid of her? I recalled how he'd talked with his cronies over the summer, and how they'd wanted her out of the way so they could use her business as a meeting place.

But could it be that simple? That horrible?

Surely, Romeo wouldn't have murdered his own sister.

Jacob and I finished our coffees, had a quick breakfast of bruschetta with his freshly made basil pesto, and then headed into Romano's to start prepping for the day.

We parked in our usual spot, and Jacob opened up while I darted across the street to chat with Matilda.

Jumbo meowed at me from inside, his fluffy white tail trembling with excitement. The bakery was already busy, the hum of chatter an accompaniment to the relief I felt over having worked things out with Jacob.

"Hello, sweetheart," I said, scooping Jumbo up into my arms. I stroked his furry head, and he bumped his little face against my hand. "Yes, aren't you the most handsome cat in the entire world?"

"Tea?" Matilda asked, heading toward the counter in the bakery.

"No, thanks," I said. "I wanted to check in and see how you're doing this morning. I was just—"

A couple of people gasped behind me, and I turned in time to witness the door to Moretti's Italian slam open down the street. Leo, the sous chef we'd interviewed at the beginning of the week, lay on the ground in front of the restaurant.

Romeo emerged from within, rolling up his sleeves and bearing down on the chef, rage all over his face.

"What on earth?" Matilda joined me. Even Jumbo stopped purring in my arms.

Romeo shouted something at Leo and aimed a kick at the man on the ground, but the sous chef rolled out of the way and scrambled upright.

"What is *wrong* with that dude?" a customer asked.

"He's got a red hot temper."

"Ever since that Moretti came to town, things have only gotten worse."

The whispers drifted through the bakery as we all watched in horror. Leo had scrambled up and hurried off down the street. Romeo looked ready to follow him, his cheeks red, but thankfully didn't.

An awful silence filled Dingle's Bakery.

"We should call the cops," Matilda whispered. "Shawn would want to know about this."

I didn't say anything. If Matilda wanted to call the police, she could, but I wasn't particularly enamored with the idea of seeing Shawn again.

"I'm going to check on Leo and see if he's OK," I said, handing Jumbo to my friend.

I exited the bakery and jogged down the street, chasing

after the sous chef. He stood near the corner, lighting up a cigarette and talking on the phone.

"Leo!" I called. "Hey, Leo!"

"Hold on a second, Mickey." He pressed a hand over the bottom of his phone and frowned at me. "Yeah?"

"Are you OK? Do you want me to call the cops?" I asked.

"Yeah nah," Leo said. "No point. They're not gonna do anything to Romeo anyway. Look, it's fine. He wants to act like a friggin' neanderthal, that's his problem. I'd like to see him get another chef as good as me any time soon. Ain't nobody gonna work for that idiot. Not after the way he treated me and the other staff. Besides, I got mine." He patted his pocket with a secretive grin.

"I'm sorry, Leo." Guilt wormed through me again. We'd turned down his application to be a sous chef at Romano's. "I can put my ear to the ground for you. See if there's any other places that are hiring."

"That's kind of you, Gina, but I'm done with this town." He gestured with his phone. "Got a buddy in the City who works at a bodega. Might need help."

"I'll leave you to it. As long as you're OK?"

"I'm good."

But as I walked away from Leo, I couldn't shake the feeling that he wasn't good, and that Romeo was up to something. Could it be murder?

Nineteen

THE REST OF THE DAY WAS LARGELY UNEVENTFUL. We opened for lunch and had several customers come in to talk about the craziness that had transpired earlier in the day.

"I'm telling you, Gina," Betty said, "he's a loose cannon. It's starting to get really alarming." Betty worked at the local doctor's office as a receptionist. She had made a name for herself with the locals as being fastidious but caring. And she had a strong moral backbone.

"I agree," I said, grasping a menu for her. I led her toward a table that looked out on the street outside. It was peaceful now, thankfully. "I'm not Romeo Moretti's biggest fan, I'll tell you that much."

"You and me both," Betty said. "Look, you know me, I was a teacher before I took on this gig at Doctor Lombardi's practice, and I can't stand it when adults behave that way. My motto is, if I wouldn't put up with it on the playground, why the heck would I put up with it in the town? Adults should behave responsibly. Just think what kind of example Romeo is setting for the folks of this town."

"It's troubling," I said.

"Even worse, he's running that restaurant again. He won't succeed, you know, not after he's gone ahead and done all of that. Kicking poor Leo to the curb. I heard he's been firing staff at the mansion too," Betty said. "Of course, that's impossible to confirm. Those Morettis like to keep to themselves. I haven't even seen that Salvatore in person. Heard he's just as bad as his son." Betty sighed and brushed her dark hair behind one ear, pursing thin lips.

She'd run out of steam, so I took the opportunity to place the menu on the table in front of her. "Can I get you anything to drink so long?" I asked.

"Oh, sure, sure. Just a milkshake. And a regular coffee." Betty always ordered two beverages minimum— variety was the spice of life, after all.

I dropped off her order with Vi, who was working the lunch shift by herself, then returned to the hostess stand at the front of the restaurant to mull over what had happened.

What am I missing?

I pulled the tablet out and laid it on the dark wood

desk, tapping my fingernails either side of it. These were strictly business hours, but the restaurant was quiet. Was there something I'd missed?

To-Do List:

- *Figure out who took the recipe book and where it could be. Retrieve it. Best place to start would be at the Moretti mansion, but how to get in there? Talk to Dolores?*
- *Find out why Dolores thinks Romeo's the one who did it. Would Romeo kill his own sister?*
- *How are Lavender and Dolores connected? Was Lavender the last one seen with Lucia or does she have an alibi?*
- *How to get the alibis? Not like they'll just outright tell me where they were. I'm not a cop.*
- *Talk to Leo again. Matilda mentioned that she saw both Romeo and Leo hanging around outside the restaurant.*

I hadn't gotten my opportunity to talk to Leo about him hanging around the restaurant, but I got the impression that the hanging around part had only been because he was desperate for a job. If what he'd said about Romeo's treatment of his staff had been true, then that made sense.

As for Lavender and Dolores, I hadn't been able to get

hold of and talk to Dolores about what had happened to her.

Why was everyone in town so unreachable? So slippery?

It seemed the only person I could talk to was Shawn, and I *did not* want to do that after the way he'd behaved the other night. *He was just doing his job.* And I had been doing my utmost best to figure things out without involving him. I could see how that would be annoying for him.

I also wasn't going to stop.

I tapped out notes on the tablet, frowning as my fingertips brushed the smooth, cool screen.

Lucia steals the recipe book. Lucia is murdered. So where is the recipe book? And why was Lucia murdered?

Lavender didn't like Lucia. Leo didn't either. Dolores didn't. Romeo could have wanted complete control of the restaurant because of his "business" dealings with shady characters.

Romeo had been driving past the restaurant repeatedly with other people in the car with him.

The front door of the restaurant opened, and I quickly tabbed out of my notes and to the reservations list, putting up a smile for our new customer.

Dolores, the Moretti's housekeeper, shuffled toward me. Today, she wore a floral skirt and brown coat that swept past her hips. Her hair was tied back in a bun, and her eyes were bloodshot as her gaze came to a rest on my face.

"Hello," she whispered.

"Dolores," I said. "Are you OK?" Concern was matched with my excitement at having her here. Maybe I could finally get some answers from her. Had she been the one to leave me the strange message?

"I—Is there somewhere we can talk privately?" she asked. "It's important."

I hesitated.

The lunch service was going smoothly, and we weren't super busy today, but it wouldn't be wise to leave the hostess station unmanned. But the temptation to talk to Dolores was too much. What if she had valuable information about what had happened to Lucia?

A sickly feeling descended on me as I considered the elderly woman in front of me. It vanished as fast as it had come.

"Of course," I said. "Just give me a second." I flagged down Vi and asked if she could watch the front while I had a chat with Dolores in the office. Afterward, I led the housekeeper through the restaurant and to the small space in the back where I had a cozy desk, two armchairs and a potted plant in the corner.

Dolores lowered herself into the chair, clutching a tote

bag in her lap. She glanced upward, almost as if she was offering up a silent prayer, then reached into her bag.

"What are you—?"

"I believe this belongs to you," Dolores whispered, and removed my uncle's top secret recipe book from her tote.

It was gorgeous, covered in red leather, the pages stained with marinara splatters, and the top printed with the golden words "RECIPE BOOK." To anyone else, this would have been just another recipe book, but to me, it was my childhood.

"Where did you get this?" I asked, taking the book from her and pressing my fingers to the soft leather cover, emotion welling inside me, clogging my throat.

A part of me had believed that I wouldn't see the book again. I'd almost given up hope after this week's events.

"Well, dear, I stole it," she said.

"Wait, what?"

Dolores dipped her head in shame. "I stole it from your house."

I was speechless.

This was the last thing I'd expected. *Goes to show how good I am at investigating.* "How? Why? Why would you do that?"

"Because Romeo Moretti asked me to."

Twenty

"BECAUSE ROMEO MORETTI ASKED ME TO."

The sentence echoed in my mind.

"Because Romeo Moretti asked me to." "Because Romeo Moretti asked me to."

With every echo, my anger grew. A white hot rage building in my veins.

"What did you just say?" I asked. "Romeo, what?"

"Romeo Moretti asked me to steal the recipe book," Dolores said. "A few weeks ago. He said that he would pay me to steal it, and that if I didn't steal it, he would fire me as the housekeeper. That he would tell Mr. Moretti, his father, that I had been stealing from the house."

"I—" I was so angry I didn't know what to say. I couldn't say anything at all. "You—"

"So I did it. I'm ashamed to say that I did as Romeo

asked me to," Dolores replied. "He stole the recipe book because he wanted to use it in the restaurant. He felt that the food wasn't good enough, and that you had an edge over Moretti's Italian."

We did, but that was beside the point.

So I'd been wrong all along about it having been Lucia. Then why on earth had she been in the tree in Jacob's back yard?

"Did Lucia know?" I asked.

"Lucia knew," she said. "Lucia wanted him to get it for her. But Romeo was the one who paid me. And now that he's fired me anyway, I'm here to return the book. I should never have taken it, and I'm sorry. If you want to call the cops on me, I'll understand."

Again, I couldn't get words out.

Romeo friggin' Moretti.

"He fired you?" I asked. "Did he fire you because you told me to come to the mansion during the memorial service?"

Confusion knit Dolores' brows together. "What message?"

So it hadn't been her who'd left me that mysterious voice message? Then who had done it? And why?

Romeo. It had to have been Romeo.

I wanted to say I couldn't believe this, but I absolutely could. The Morettis had been breaking rules ever since they set foot in Lake Basil. This was just another part of their show of "dominance." And I was done with it.

So done with it I could barely think straight.

"Would you tell the cops about what Romeo asked you to do?" I asked. "If I called them?"

"Yes," Dolores said. "But there's more."

"More?"

"I'm sure that Romeo's the one that killed Lucia," Dolores said. "When I stole the recipe book and brought it to him, he refused to give it to her. They got in a huge fight over it and they sent me home. The next day, when I arrived to go to work, Lucia was dead. I think their fight must've gotten physical." She had gone pale at the thought.

The more I thought about it, the more it made sense. The recipe book being stolen. Romeo's descent into madness over the past couple of weeks.

"Romeo's changed since I was hired," Dolores said. "He was always mean, Lucia too, but he's grown more controlling. He told me that Lucia was running the restaurant into the ground. That the chefs had no idea what they were doing, and that it was Lucia's fault because she was the one in control of the menu. And then Lucia was threatening to fire them all and Romeo started trying to step in and take control." The words poured out of Dolores. It was like she couldn't stop herself from talking now that it had happened. "I—I'm sure it was him."

The note she'd given me had said as much.

"All right," I said. "But what about Lavender McGee?"

Dolores frowned. "What about her?"

"She attacked you, didn't she?"

"Yeah, years ago. And that was just because she lost her temper at the grocery store. It has nothing to do with this."

I hesitated. "Dolores, I'm going to need you to go down to the police station and tell them all of this." I rose from my seat.

"But what are you going to do?" she asked.

"Me? I'm going to have a quick chat with Romeo."

BAD IDEA OR NOT, I WASN'T GOING TO LET Romeo Moretti get away with this. I sent Jacob a quick text and let him know where I was going—as much as I wanted to rely on him in this context, I didn't want to disturb him while he was busy with his shift in the kitchen.

I marched from the restaurant and down the sidewalk. Passersby jumped out of my path at the look on my face, many of them whispering behind their hands or looking downright terrified.

My purse was slung over my shoulder, my pepper spray ready for use if Romeo decided to do anything untoward.

I opened the door to Moretti's Italian, and a fresh wave of anger hit me. I'd forgotten just how similar this place looked to Romano's.

It was like the Moretti's had snapped a picture of our restaurant and bought everything they could find to match it. The white tablecloths. THe brick walls. The crystal glasses, the green carpeting and hanging potted plants. Even the music was similar.

But the place was empty inside. And Moretti's didn't smell of anything today. Not even burned garlic—maybe that was because Leo had been fired.

"Romeo!" I yelled.

The server who'd been lazing near the hostess stand nearly jumped out of her skin. "What the—?"

"Romeo, you get your butt out here right now!"

The doors to the kitchen swung open and Romeo emerged, wearing a chef's hat and an apron that was covered in splatters of sauce. His eyes were red and watering—cutting onions? Crying over the fact that his sister was dead?

No, it had to be the former. Dolores was convinced Romeo was the killer.

Romeo held a knife in one hand and he gestured with

it, shedding a slice of onion from the end of the silver blade. "What the heck are you doing here? You outta your mind? You don't come into my restaurant and—"

"Don't you dare talk to me like that!" I whipped my pepper spray out of my bag. If he could have a knife. I could have the spray. "I know you stole my recipe book."

Romeo lost steam real quick. "Don't know what you're talking about. Didn't do anything."

"I know that you had Dolores steal the recipe book," I snapped. "And she's on her way to the cops to tell them as much."

"Hey, whoa, hey," Romeo said, putting the knife down. "See? I'm not doing anything. Let's talk about this."

"Oh, now you want to talk," I said, my gaze fell to the knife. "Now, you want to—" The knife.

The knife.

The knife.

The knife's hilt that bore the sweeping "M" for the Moretti family.

"What are you—You having a stroke or something?" Romeo asked. "You're sweating."

I glared at him, but the bite was gone. My anger faded to fear. "Romeo," I said, "where does that knife come from?"

"This one?" he asked. "It's from the kitchen."

"The restaurant kitchen?"

"Yeah. What's that got to—?"

"Are all the knives in the kitchen like that?" It made sense. How hadn't I seen it before? The kitchen knives at the Moretti mansion, the block that had held them had been full. None of those knives had been missing.

"Like what?"

"Engraved with the letter 'M'?"

"Oh, yeah." Romeo's chest puffed outward. "Of course. Why wouldn't they—?"

I turned on my heel and darted out of the restaurant, back down the street and into Romano's. "Jacob! Jacob, I need your help!"

Twenty-One

"I DON'T KNOW ABOUT THIS, GINA," JACOB SAID. "I can't just let you go on your own." He stood in front of the stove, apron still on, with Ross nearby listening in on our conversation. The other chefs weren't as concerned about it, keeping to themselves as they prepared pizzas and pastas for our lunch guests.

"I have to go now," I said. "Now. I tried to call Shawn, but he's not picking up. Leo could be gone by now."

Jacob glanced over at Ross. The sous chef gave the barest hint of a nod, and then Jacob stripped off his apron and hung it on the hook behind the kitchen door. He grabbed hold of my arm and walked me out into the dining area.

"Jacob, I—"

"Get in the car," he said. "I'm coming with you. Call 911. Do you know where he lives?"

"Yeah," I said. "His resume. I still have it on the tablet." I snatched the tablet up from the hostess station as we made our way out. My gaze moved across the restaurant, but it was mostly empty, and Violet had everything under control.

She gave me a thumbs up when she saw us heading for the door.

"This is a bad idea," Jacob said, "but I'm not going to let you make it on your own." He hustled me into the car and then started the engine.

I tried Shawn's number one more time then sent him a text.

Leo is the killer. He used the knife from the kitchen at the restaurant. He's going to leave town for the City. We're going to stop him.

I sent it as a courtesy and then called 911.

THE DRIVE OVER TO LEO'S PLACE—A TRAILER IN the park on Granner Way—was taken at breakneck speed. Jacob stayed focused on the road, while I kept my eyes on my phone, hoping that Shawn would send me a text or at least call me back. The dispatcher on the other end of the line had taken my "tip" and said she'd given it to the local police.

I'd neglected to tell her that we were currently en route to Leo's place. The cops didn't need to know that.

Our goal was to stop Leo before he got out of Lake Basil.

We couldn't let him escape.

The puzzle pieces had finally clicked into place in my mind.

The Morettis, Lucia especially, had treated their employees poorly. Leo had been afraid of telling us where he worked. Lucia had been in control of the menu, had stopped him from cooking what he wanted, she had bullied him, just like Romeo had bullied Dolores.

And Leo had snapped.

That was the only explanation for it. He had snapped when she had fired him because Romeo must have *told* Lucia that Leo had been interviewing for the position of sous chef at our restaurant.

The thought made me sick.

If we'd never interviewed Leo or if we'd maybe accepted him as the sous chef...

But no, he hadn't been good enough. And imagine we had accepted him and he'd wound up killing one of the staff at Romano's instead.

This is a nightmare.

And the murder weapon? Straight from the kitchen.

No wonder Shawn had asked me how I'd known it had come from the kitchen at the beginning of the week. But if Shawn knew about that, then why hadn't he just up and arrested Leo already? What more proof did he need for—

Jacob took the corner at high speed and skidded to a halt in front of the entrance to the trailer park.

Police cars filled the street, blocking it and the dirt path that led into the trailer park and wound past campers and trailers alike.

A commotion had broken out.

Shawn had "decentralized" someone on the floor.

"I think they've got him," Jacob said.

"But how? How did they know?"

Shawn brought the suspect to his feet, and Leo, red-cheeked and glaring around, left and right, was marched toward the back of a squad car. Shawn caught sight of us and shook his head, gesturing for us to get out of here.

"How did he know?" I repeated. "Why didn't he arrest Leo sooner?"

"I don't know, Gina, but we'd better get out of here before we get in real trouble." Jacob put the car in reverse and brought us back onto the road. We drove back toward the restaurant, and I sat in the passenger seat, frustrated at not having solved this sooner.

It had been difficult, though.

There had been several suspects. And what about the whole thing with Lavender and Dolores? And with Lavender and her anger at Lucia?

I sighed and pinched the bridge of my nose. I couldn't possibly have known that the knives at Moretti's Italian were the same as the ones at the mansion. And the voice message? That had to have come from Moretti.

A text message blipped through on my cell phone just as we pulled into the parking space in front of the restaurant.

"Is it Shawn?" Jacob asked.

I lifted my phone and nodded. I read the text out to him. "Thanks for the help. The reason I was out at the Moretti's the other night was because we'd set up an operation to lure Leo out there. We figured he'd want to take down Romeo too."

"That's it?" Jacob asked. "Why didn't they arrest him sooner?"

"Maybe they didn't have enough," I said. "I don't get it either, Jake."

Another text. "I'm only telling you this because you... helped. But we didn't have enough evidence to take him down until he was fired from Moretti's and stole a knife from the restaurant. When Romeo reported it stolen, we had enough for a warrant. We searched his house and found bloody clothing. DNA matched Lucia's."

I typed out my thanks to Shawn, even though he'd irritated me to no end when he'd followed us home.

"Only reason I followed you both home was because I didn't want Leo to attack you next," Shawn said. "I had reason to believe he was watching you. We were monitoring his calls and one of them went out to your number."

That explained the voice message I'd received.

My skin crawled.

Jacob reached over and grabbed my hand, squeezing it tight. "It's OK," he said. "It's over now."

I was overwhelmed with gratitude. We were safe, Shawn had caught the killer, and the recipe book was back in my possession. This had to have been the worst start to fall ever, but Lucia's family could have peace in the fact that the killer had been caught.

Life could return to normal in Lake Basil. Or at least a semblance of it.

Twenty-Two

Two weeks later...

JACOB WORE AN APRON THAT MY AUNT HAD brought over especially for him. It was striped red, white and green and bore the words "Romano by Choice" printed across the front pocket. It was cute, but it was also a very obvious hint that she wanted Jacob and I to get married already.

And that was a step that was still far in the future. Wasn't it?

I topped up my aunt's glass of red wine, and she gave me a special smile from where she leaned her head on Uncle Rocco's shoulder.

Jacob hummed as he chopped vegetables for tonight's farfalle dish, while Uncle Rocco regaled us with tales of his time in the restaurant. The stereo on the corner countertop played soft background music, and a glance out of the kitchen window showed the setting sun over the lake's surface. Life had returned to normal.

Better than normal.

"And then she said to me," Uncle Rocco said, "she said that if I didn't make her a fresh margarita pizza right away, she wouldn't be coming back to the pizzeria."

"So what did you say?" Matilda sat opposite my aunt and uncle, a tall glass of sparkling water in front of her and Jumbo seated in her lap, purring as she stroked him. He was a good cat, and he didn't mind walks on his leash, so a trip to our house didn't upset him.

"What did I say?" Uncle Rocco laughed, a belly-shaking laugh that filled the room with warmth.

Jacob shot me a smile from in front of the stove followed by a wink.

My heart did a little flip, and I blew him a kiss in return.

"I told her that if she was so desperate for a margarita, she could go on ahead and make one herself," Rocco said. "That or pick the pepperoni off the pizza."

"And then I said that the only way I'd pick pepperoni off the pizza," Aunt Sofia put in, "was if he ate the pepperoni for me."

"It was a fun night," Uncle Rocco said, with a misty-eyed look. "Sofia was beautiful."

"*Was* beautiful?" Aunt Sof whapped my uncle on the arm. "What kind of bonehead thing is that to say?"

"Aw, come on, Sof, of course you're still beautiful." Rocco kissed the top of her head. "Just as beautiful as the day I met you."

"One day," Matilda said, "I'm going to have a relationship like yours. Or at the very least, Jumbo will have a relationship like yours with the cat down the street."

Laughter filled the kitchen.

"Almost done," Jacob called, as he pulled plates out of the cupboard and started getting ready to dish up.

"Do you need help?" Uncle Rocco shifted.

"No, no, I've got it. You guys relax."

A knock rattled the front door, and I frowned. I couldn't imagine who it would be. Everyone I loved was here. "I'll be right back," I said, and left the bustling kitchen full of my favorite people.

I walked through to the front hall and checked through the newly installed peephole. Nobody was out there.

A thrill of alarm ran down my spine, but I shook it off.

This was ridiculous. The murderer was behind bars. And Lake Basil was safe again. Sure, the Morettis hadn't left town, but I doubted they'd do anything to me, not after I'd told Romeo I'd press charges over the recipe book theft if he tried anything.

I opened the front door and looked around.

A single rose lay on the welcome mat, a square white card secured to its stem with a ribbon.

I picked up the rose, full of confusion. "I'm not done with you yet." That was what the card said. Just that, written in looping text. I turned it over and found the letters "S.C." on the back.

"Seriously?" I murmured.

Shawn had left me a rose? That was so inappropriate.

"Gina?" Jacob called. "Dinner's ready. Who's at the door?"

I crumpled up the card and shoved it in my pocket for later disposal, then tossed the rose into the bushes at the side of our house. "Nobody," I called.

And then I shut the door tight and returned to my loved ones, the beginnings of worry building in my stomach. I didn't know what Shawn was playing at, but he'd lost it if he thought he could interfere in my relationship with Jacob.

I sat down at the kitchen table beside my boyfriend and looped my fingers through his. "Thank you," I said. "This looks great."

"Anything for you." He pressed a kiss to my forehead, and I smiled at him, the card in my pocket forgotten, and the start of the rest of our lives written in the gentle expression in his eyes.

Will Gina get over her fear of commitment and settle down with Jacob, or is the secret surprise that Shawn Carter's planning enough to make her change her mind. Find out by reading The Farfalle Fatality!

Craving More Cozy Mystery?

If you had fun with Ruby and Bee, you'll, love getting to know Charlie Mission and her butt-kicking grandmother, Georgina. You can read the first chapter of Charlie's story, *The Case of the Waffling Warrants,* below!

"Come in, Big G, come in." I spoke under my breath so that the flesh-colored microphone seated against my throat picked up my voice. "What is your status?"

My grandmother, Georgina—pet name Gamma, code name Big G—was out on a special operation. Reconnaissance at the newest guesthouse in our town, Gossip. The reason? First, she was an ex-spy, as was I, and second, the woman who'd opened the guesthouse was her mortal enemy and in direct competition with my grandmother's establishment, the Gossip Inn.

Who was this enemy, this bringer of potential financial doom?

A middle-aged woman with a penchant for wearing pashminas and annoying anyone who looked her way.

Jessie Belle-Blue.

It was rumored that even thinking the woman's name summoned a murder of crows.

"I repeat, Big G, what is your status?"

"I'm en route to the nest," my grandmother replied in my earpiece.

I let out a relieved sigh and exited my bedroom, heading downstairs to help with the breakfast service.

In the nine months since I had retired as a spy, life in Gossip had been normal. In the Gossip sense of the term. I'd expected that my job as a server, maid, and assistant would bring the usual level of "cat herding" inherent when working at the inn. Whether that involved tracking down runaway cats, literally, or providing a guest with a moist towelette after a fainting spell—tempers ran high in Gossip.

What was the reason for the craziness? Shoot, it had to be something in the water.

I took the main stairs two at a time and found my friend, the inn's chef, paging through her recipe book in the lime green kitchen. Lauren Harris wore her red hair in a French braid today, apron stretched over her pregnant belly.

"Morning," I said, "how are you today?"

"Madder than a fat cat on a diet." She slapped her recipe book closed and turned to me.

Uh oh. Looks like it's time for more cat herding.

"What's wrong?"

"My supplier is out of flour and sugar. Can you believe that?" Lauren huffed, smoothing her hands over her belly while the clock on the wall ticked away. Breakfast was in two hours and Lauren loved baking cupcakes as part of the meal.

"Do you have enough supplies to make cupcakes for this morning?"

"Yes. But just for today," Lauren replied. "The guests are going to love my new waffle cupcakes, and they'll be sore they can't get anymore after this batch is done. Why, I should go down there and wring Billy's neck for doing this to me. He knows I take an order of sugar and flour every week, and I get it at just above cost too. What's Georgina going to say?"

"Don't stress, Lauren," I said. "We'll figure it out."

"Right." She brightened a little. "I nearly forgot you're the one who "fixes" things around here." Lauren winked at me.

She was the only person in the entire town who knew that my grandmother and I had once been spies for the NSIB—the National Security Investigative Bureau. But the news that I had helped solve several murders had spread through town, and now, anybody and everybody with a problem would call me up asking for help. A lot of them offered me money. And I was selective about who I chose to help.

"I'll check it out for you if you'd like," I said. "The flour issue."

"Nah, that's OK. I'm sure Billy will get more stock this week. I'll lean on him until he squeals."

"Sounds like you've been picking up tips from Georgina."

Lauren giggled then returned to her super-secret recipe book—no one but she was allowed to touch it.

"What's on the menu this morning?" I asked.

Lauren was the boss in the kitchen—she told me what to do, and I followed her instructions precisely. If I did anything else, like trying to read the recipe for instance, the food would end up burned, missing ingredients or worse.

The only place I wasn't a "fixer" was in the Gossip Inn's kitchen.

"Bacon and eggs over easy, biscuits and gravy, waffle cupcakes and... oh, I can't make fresh baked bread, can I?"

"Tell her I'll bring some back with me from the

bakery." Gamma's voice startled me. Goodness, I'd forgotten about the earpiece—she could hear everything happening in the kitchen.

"I'll text Georgina and ask her to bring bread from the bakery."

"You're a lifesaver, Charlotte."

We set to work on the breakfast—it was 7:00 a.m. and we needed everything done within two hours—and fell into our easy rhythm of baking and cooking.

My grandmother entered the kitchen at around 8:30 a.m., dressed in a neat silk blouse and a pair of slacks rather than the black outfit she'd left in for her spy mission. Tall, willowy, and with neatly styled gray hair, Gamma had always reminded me of Helen Mirren playing the Queen.

"Good morning, ladies," she said, in her prim, British accent. "I bring bread and tidings."

"What did you find out?" I asked.

"No evidence of the supposed ghost tours," Gamma said.

We'd started hosting ghost tours at the inn recently, so of course Jessie Belle-Blue wanted to do the same. She was all about under-cutting us, but, thankfully, the Gossip Inn had a legacy and over 1,000 positive reviews on Trip-Advisor.

Breakfast time arrived, and the guests filled the quaint dining area with its glossy tables, creaking wooden floors, and egg yolk yellow walls. Chatter and laughter leaked through the swinging kitchen doors with their porthole windows.

"That's my cue," I said, dusting off my apron, and heading out into the dining room.

I picked up a pot of coffee from the sideboard where we kept the drinks station and started my rounds.

Most of the guests had gathered around a center table in the dining room, and bursts of laughter came from the group, accompanied by the occasional shout.

I elbowed my way past a couple of guests—nobody could accuse me of having great people skills—apologizing along the way until I reached the table. The last time something like this had happened, a murder had followed shortly afterward.

Not this time. No way.

"—the last thing she'd ever hear!" The woman seated at the table, drawing the attention, was vaguely familiar. She wore her dark hair in luscious curls, and tossed it as she spoke, looking down her upturned nose at the people around the table.

"What happened then, Mandy?" Another woman asked, her hands clasped together in front of her stomach.

Mandy? Wait a second, isn't this Mandy Gilmore?

Gamma had mentioned her once before—Mandy was

a massive gossip in town. Why wasn't she staying at her house?

"What happened? Well, she ran off with her tail between her legs, of course. She'll soon learn not to cross me. Heaven knows, I always repay my debts."

"What, like a Lannister from *Game of Thrones*?" That had come from a taller woman with ginger curls.

"Shut up, Opal," Mandy replied. "You have no idea what we're talking about, and even if you did, you wouldn't have the intelligence to comprehend it."

The crowd let out various 'oofs' in response to that. The woman next to me clapped her hand over her mouth.

"You're all talk, Gilmore." Opal lifted a hand and yammered it at the other woman. "You act like you're a threat, but we know the truth around here."

"The truth?" Mandy leaned in, pressing her hands flat onto the tabletop, the crystal vase in the center rattling. "And what's that, Opal, darling? I'd love to hear it."

"That you're a failure. You sold your house, left Gossip with your head in the clouds, told everyone you were going to become a successful businesswoman, and now you're back. Back to scrape together the pieces of the life you have left."

"Witch!" Mandy scraped her chair back.

"All right, all right," I said, setting down the coffee pot

on the table. "That's enough, ladies. Everyone head back to their tables before things get out of hand."

Both Opal and Mandy stared daggers at me.

I flashed them both smiles. "We wouldn't want to ruin breakfast, would we? Lauren's prepared waffle cupcakes."

That distracted them. "Waffle cupcakes?" Opal's brow wrinkled. "How's that going to work?"

"Let's talk about it at your table." I grabbed my coffee pot and walked her away from Mandy. The crowd slowly dispersed, people muttering regret at having missed out on a show. The Gossip Inn was popular for its constant conflict.

If the rumors didn't start here then they weren't worth repeating. That was the mantra, anyway.

I seated Opal at her table, and she pursed her lips at me. "You shouldn't have interrupted. That woman needs a piece of my mind."

"We prefer peace of mind at the inn." I put up another of my best smiles.

Compared to what I'd been through in the past—hiding out from my rogue spy ex-husband and eventually helping put him behind bars when he found me—dealing with the guests was a cakewalk.

"What brings you to Gossip, Opal?" I asked.

"I live here," she replied, waspishly. "I'm staying here while they're fumigating my house. Roaches."

"Ah." I struggled not to grimace. Thankfully, my cell phone buzzed in the front pocket of my apron and distracted me. "Coffee?"

"I don't take caffeine." And she said it like I'd offered her an illegal substance too.

"Call me if you need anything." I hurried off before she could make good on that promise, bringing my phone out of my pocket.

I left the coffee pot on the sideboard, moving into the Gossip Inn's spacious foyer, the chandelier overhead off, but catching light in glimmers. The tables lining the hall were filled with trinkets from the days when the inn had been a museum—an eclectic collection of bits and bobs.

"This is Charlotte Smith," I answered the call—I would never get to use my true last name, Mission, again, but it was safer this way.

"Hello, Charlotte." A soft, rasping voice. "I've been trying to get through to you. I'm desperate."

"Who is this?"

"My name is Tina Rogers, and I need your help."

"My help."

"Yes," she said. "I understand that you have a certain set of skills. That you fix people's problems?"

"I do. But it depends on the problem and the price." I didn't have a set fee for helping people, but if it drew me away from the inn for long, I had to charge. I was technically a consultant now. Sort of like a P.I. without the fedora and coffee-stained shirt.

"My mother will handle your fee," Tina said. "I've asked her to text you about it, but I... I don't have long to talk. They're going to pull me off the phone soon."

"Who?"

"The police," she replied. "I'm calling you from the holding cell at the Gossip Police Station. I've been arrested on false charges, and I need you to help me prove my innocence."

"Miss Rogers, it's probably a better idea to invest in a lawyer." But I was tempted. It had been a long time since I'd felt useful.

"No! I'm not going to a lawyer. I'm going to make these idiots pay for ever having arrested me."

I took a breath. "OK. Before I accept your... case, I'll need to know what happened. You'll need to tell me everything." I glanced through the open doorway that led into the dining room. No one looked unhappy about the lack of service yet.

"I can't tell you everything now. I don't have much time."

"So give me the *CliffsNotes*."

"I was arrested for breaking into and vandalizing Josie Carlson's bakery, The Little Cake Shop. Apparently, they found my glove there—it was specially embroidered, you see—but it's not mine because—" The line went dead.

"Hello? Miss Rogers?" I pulled the cellphone away from my ear and frowned at the screen. "Darn."

My interest was piqued. A mystery case about a break-in that involved the local bakery? Which just so happened to be run by one of my least favorite people in Gossip?

And when I'd just started getting bored with the push and pull of everyday life at the inn?

Count me in.

Want to read more? You can grab **the first book** in *the Gossip Cozy Mystery series* on all major retailers.

Happy reading, friend!

Paperbacks Available by Rosie A. Point

A Burger Bar Mystery series

The Fiesta Burger Murder

The Double Cheese Burger Murder

The Chicken Burger Murder

The Breakfast Burger Murder

The Salmon Burger Murder

The Cheesy Steak Burger Murder

A Bite-sized Bakery Cozy Mystery series

Murder by Chocolate

Marzipan and Murder

Creepy Cake Murder

Murder and Meringue Cake

Murder Under the Mistletoe

Murder Glazed Donuts

Choc Chip Murder

Macarons and Murder

Candy Cake Murder

Murder by Rainbow Cake

Murder With Sprinkles

Trick or Murder

Christmas Cake Murder

S'more Murder

Murder and Marshmallows

Donut Murder

Buttercream Murder

Chocolate Cherry Murder

Caramel Apple Murder

Red, White 'n Blue Murder

Pink Sprinkled Murder

Murder by Milkshake

Murder by Cupid Cake

Caramel Cupcake Murder

Cake Pops and Murder

A Milly Pepper Mystery series

Maple Drizzle Murder

A Sunny Side Up Cozy Mystery series

Murder Over Easy

Muffin But Murder

Chicken Murder Soup

Murderoni and Cheese

Lemon Murder Pie

A Gossip Cozy Mystery series

The Case of the Waffling Warrants

The Case of the Key Lime Crimes

The Case of the Custard Conspiracy

The Case of the Butterscotch Burglars

A Mission Inn-possible Cozy Mystery series

Vanilla Vendetta

Strawberry Sin

Cocoa Conviction

Mint Murder

Raspberry Revenge

Chocolate Chills

A Very Murder Christmas series

Dachshund Through the Snow

Owl Be Home for Christmas

A Pizza Parlor Cozy Mystery series

Slice of Murder

Murder Boxed Up

Hold the Murder

Dough Not Murder

Made in the USA
Las Vegas, NV
20 January 2025

16719817R00094